LEDRA

 NORA NADJA... Cyprus. She has published three collections of poetry, and has been awarded prizes in various international competitions, including the Scottish International Open Poetry Competition (2000 and 2003), the Plough Arts Centre Poetry Competition (2003), Poetry on the Lake (2005) and the Féile Filiochta Poetry Competition (2005).

Her second poetry collection *Cleft in Twain* was one of the books from Cyprus recommended in an article in *The Guardian* on the literature of the new member states of the European Union (1st May 2004). Her work was also included in *May Day: Young Literature from the Ten New Member States of the European Union* (published by the European Commission).

Shorter versions of 'Ledra Street' and 'No-Man's-Land' were Highly Commended in the Commonwealth Short Story Competition in 2001 and 2005 respectively. 'Spoon Sweet' was Highly Commended in the same competition in 2002.

Extracts from 'Ledra Street' were used in a documentary on Cyprus by Austrian Television ORF/3sat. The programme was part of the series "CONNECT EUROPA" and was broadcast in Europe in December 2001.

By NORA NADJARIAN

The Voice at the Top of the Stairs
Cleft in Twain
25 ways to kiss a man

NORA NADJARIAN

LEDRA STREET

Stories

Armida

Published by Armida Publications 2006

Some of the stories in this collection have previously appeared in
Dream Catcher, Gallerie, In Our Own Words (Vol.6),
Orbis, Orphan Leaf Review, Staple, the-phone-book
and Creativity in Exile (Rodopi)

ISBN 9963-620-43-4

Cover Photograph © Thodoris Tzalavras 2006

Printed and bound by Regal Printing Ltd, Hong Kong

With the kind support of the Cultural Services,
Ministry of Education and Culture
of the Republic of Cyprus

Armida Publications
P.O.Box 27717, 2432 Engomi, Nicosia, Cyprus

www.armidapublications.com

for N.
with love

CONTENTS

Ledra Street

I would like to tell you about the kafenion, about the cat that lived there, and the cheese rinds I fed it. About the coffee-shop owner who was hit by a car, and the tray and glasses and the coffee which flew. These are the less important things.

More importantly, there was a time Ledra street was whole, non-pedestrianised, and we still called Turkish coffee, Turkish. But that was a long time ago.

I can find the spot even now where the coffee-shop owner tried to cross, and the car hit him and the glass and the cups and the coffee flew. He died in hospital later. The tyres screeched, the men gathered round and my father ran out of his shop with a pic-measure in his hand to see if it was me, panic written in his eyes and a pic-measure in his hands, as if to measure the life or death left in the body on the tarmac. I read panic again in my father's eyes one hot July day, the day I grew up. The day my memory was divided into important and less important things.

Today I walked on Ledra Street and counted the steps from where the kafenion stood, all the way to the checkpoint. It was fifty-two steps. Fifty-two steps to freedom, fifty-two steps to captivity. I can only imagine the other side. My father's shop hidden in a souk. Labyrinths of spices, hands dripping gold, a tree of idleness, Bellapaix, la belle paix. When the hodja's voice clings to the clammy summer evenings, I try to imagine his face and weigh the importance of his syllables. What is he asking God, and how carefully is God listening?

I secretly mourned the coffee-shop owner's death for years. It was my fault he died. 'Don't feed it on the table,' he would say. 'Not on the table. A cat has nine, I have only one. If anyone comes in and finds a cat on the table in my kitchen, I will not have any custom. I will not have a life.' And the day he lost his life, he made three coffees on the pale blue flame. The bubbles of the coffee rose and subsided, rose and subsided in the 'brikki'. He lined up the little cups, filled them, picked up the aluminium tray, that special swaying pyramid of a tray, and left his shop, the cat, and me.

It was my fault. I would like to say this to the sky in the evening, like the hodja: it was my fault. But somehow it doesn't seem important any more. It sounds silly, even. I had been feeding the cat on the table, when I thought I heard a noise. I took the cat and threw it on the floor. Frightened, it ran into the street and got tangled in his feet. The brakes screeched, too late. So he died, because of me and a stupid cat.

It was in the paper the next day. My father made his lips small enough to pull in the coffee from the little cup, and read – possibly to himself, possibly to my mother: 'Andreas Demetriou, 41, killed by driver on Ledra street.' My mother said: 'And his wife? And his children? Don't they ever write about those that are left behind?'

I am now the one left behind. Behind a wall, behind a checkpoint, looking for my father's shop, looking for my childhood, dismissing a man's death, mourning the division of a city. Counting the steps to the other side. Wondering where unimportance ends and importance begins.

A bride is coming out of church, smiling. It is my mother. I will not mention the groom, only the bride. She looks serene, like a sylph, as if she knows she has a long way to go. Around her is noise of happiness, a crowd of well-wishers, an admiration of bridesmaids (a flock of birds, a pride of lions, an admiration of bridesmaids) as if she has a long, long way to go. And she does, only she doesn't know it yet. Behind her the church which now exists only in dreams which she now sees only in dreams, except that it still exists only a few metres away but she cannot reach it. 'It was Victoria street and we were happy. I was seventeen years old and I was happy because my life was changing, getting bigger. And there was love. Church bells rang and there was a love of God, the hodja sang in the minaret and there was love for God. And suddenly overnight everyone hated each other.'

In the photograph they smile, not at each other but at the photographer. Anyone can see that they are strangers, that it is an arranged marriage, that love is absent from the photo, that my mother's frozen smile is really a sigh in disguise.

One wall in the kafenion, on the left as you went in, was covered in telephone numbers written in pencil. Just that one wall was a wall-telephone directory. I would stand beneath it, cock my head up and read all the names and numbers written in scrawls of different sizes, until I found I was looking too far up and felt dizzy. Yiannis 34457, Sotiris 46734, long lists of men's names mostly, some faded away with time. Standing on a chair once, I found a woman's name: Maria, near the top. The small word and number were hidden, in fact, under a framed picture of a young red-haired woman wearing a blue dress. The woman had an immense bust and looked almost like an amazon. 'What a child! God, what a child!' said Andreas the coffee shop owner, coming in with the tray, seeing me standing on the chair. 'Get down, will you? And go and play in your father's shop.' He straightened the picture frame so the woman's name wouldn't show. 'That's Sophia. Leave her alone.' I thought he would say 'That's Maria' but he didn't. 'She's an actress. See if you can grow up to be as pretty as her!' With a laugh, he pushed the chair aside and disappeared into the kitchen. I could hear him whistling. He always whistled when he was happy.

Whenever I see a picture of Sophia Loren, I always remember the coffee shop and that hidden name, Maria.

If you walk along Regina street you will find hundreds of Marias waiting for a phone call from Andreas, or Kostas, or Stelios. She waited and waited – smoked a cigarette and waited, painted her fingernails and waited, refused other custom and waited.

It had been arranged that they would meet that night, but he didn't call. She had a drink, put on her new dress and left in a hurry, as if her whole life depended on finding out why Andreas hadn't rung. If she walked towards the coffee shop (she had done it once before, and he had asked her not to. Too many people know me here, he had told her …)

Peering in the dark, she looked to see him, but the place was shut, the door bolted, a silence hanging like the black night. Next time, she would ask him for the key. And as she crossed the street to walk back to Regina street, she stepped on a recently dried stain of blood which looked black in the night.

'*Andreas Demetriou, 41, killed by driver on Ledra street.*'

Guided Tour

Somewhere, the street ends, and another part of it begins. Greek side, Turkish side and in the middle a partition, and a young guard with a rifle pacing up and down. HALT. Don't cross over. YOU ARE NOT ALLOWED TO CROSS OVER. NOT ALLOWED. NO PHOTOGRAPHY. HALT. CAPITAL LETTERS ARE IMPORTANT WHEN YOU ARE FORBIDDING PEOPLE. DON'T MOVE FROM ONE HALF TO THE OTHER. OR FROM THE OTHER HALF TO THIS. This is where Ledra street ends. This is where the freedom of your steps ends. The guard paces up and down, up and down. And wishes he could smoke a cigarette. Above his head the sign reads NOTHING IS GAINED WITHOUT SACRIFICE.

Ladies and gentlemen, says the tourist guide, Welcome to Nicosia. The Last Divided Capital in the World.

The group of British tourists are exactly on time, half past three on the dot, for their guided tour of Nicosia. Six middle-aged and three young couples and three children. Frosso greets them and gives them her hearty but empty Welcome To Cyprus speech which lulls them into thinking in the early afternoon heat that they are important, they are seeing places, they are now in the divided capital, they will tell their friends all about it back home. Cameras flash.

Welcome to Cyprus – Welcome to Nicosia, the last divided capital in the world. On your left – On your right – As you can see – You can just make out – Round the corner – Not far from here – Here, in Cyprus – the Turkish invasion – the situation – the Laiki Geitonia – half an hour, then, in the tourist shops –

The driver parks his air-conditioned coach and asks Frosso when they will be back. Half and hour, she says. Enough time for your cigarette Mr Kosta, she smiles. Mr Kostas the driver takes his packet of Rothmans and his matches and worry beads out of his pocket and waits for the tourists to get off. He smiles at the young woman with the blond pony tail holding a five-year-old version of herself by the hand. They are the last to get off. The father got off earlier, a video camera on his shoulder, a rucksack on his back.

Come on, come on, Mandy, says the woman wearing the strapless top and shorts, proudly displaying a deep, dark tan. Oh sorry! she exclaims when Mandy pulls at an icon of Ayios Demetrios stuck on the dashboard. OK, OK, says Mr Kostas, picking the icon off the floor. I'm so sorry! says the young mother. Ok, ok, is nothing says Mr Kostas and is proud of himself for managing to convey an extraordinarily wide range of emotions with a very limited vocabulary: OK. Nothing. No problem. Thank you, thank you. Please. Sorry. Bus. Come. Bye bye. Hello. The woman smiles at him and says thank you, to which he replies Please.

Please now look to your right, says Frosso, where you can see Famagusta Gate, one of the three gates of the walls of Nicosia. It is considered by many to be the capital's finest surviving Venetian monument. It was one of the three original entrances to the old city of Nicosia, and it was named Famagusta Gate because of its position east of the walls, serving mainly the roads from the Famagusta and Larnaca districts.

Ten pairs of eyes, the keenest, watch Frosso and then turn to the Gate with its hue of gold in the early afternoon light.

Somebody asks when it was built.

1567, says Frosso.

1567! The date resonates with the weight of time, more time than is conceivable, more time than is possible to imagine.

The Gate is mentioned, says Frosso, in descriptions of the siege of Nicosia by the Turks in 1570. It was the only way out for the besieged from within the wall, as fighting was taking place around the nearby bastions.

Ah, says an elderly Englishman, whose knowledge of Cypriot history only goes back to the 1955-59 EOKA struggle. His face has gone pink in the sun, and under his straw hat it is an arched Ah, like his eyebrows, as if he understands everything now. Everything makes perfect sense. Of course, of course, history when it becomes history, when it can be read in history books, when it can be talked about by tourist guides, makes perfect sense. The only way out.

The only way out, Frosso also thinks, as soon as she has said the words. What a strange thing, a rare pain, to be trapped in your own country. The only way out, now, is what? Where? Do you understand? she wants to ask them. Do you really understand what it's like? She remembers a poem she once had to learn off by heart at school. The Walls, K. P. Kavafis. 'The city will follow you. And you will grow old in the same streets, in the same neighbourhoods …' The city will follow you, and remind you every day that you are trapped in the south. That there is also a north, 'another side', beyond the checkpoints. That north and south don't necessarily mix and years change and some facts stay the same. History only changes drastically and beautifully from page to page in history books.

The tourists look and listen like good pupils who will score highly in the history test. They will revise all the important dates, memorise them and even remember them for a while, and then, inevitably, one day, soon, under a cold, grey sky all those warm holiday feelings will be gone. The dates will fly away, and there will be the snapshots of the cheap mid-winter package beaches at Agia Napa to look at and admire. The blue sea, blue sky, the I LOVE CYPRUS T-shirts and the almost tan.

At sunset, the city is gold. The light is still strong and, for the tourists, exotic. The dark outlines of the houses, high-rise buildings, churches, palm trees and mosques, all merge as in a shadow theatre. A stage set under the sun, the city is one. But.

What a strange way to live, says one tourist to the other. Half a city.

The sweetness of the coming evening is heart rending. It pulls at the light, the gold darkens. And in the sky a silence. Half light, half dark.

Half city.

Flamingoes

Summer comes too soon in Cyprus, burns all the other seasons. If you listen, you can hear the heat crackling. My grandmother used to say I was a summer child, always playing with fire. Perhaps that is why when the water evaporates and a thin crust of pure salt remains in the salt lake, I dream of the flamingoes. They come every year, like flames in the blue sky, setting my imagination alight. Once a year, the serene salt lake in Larnaca is alive.

The salt lake was a curse from Saint Lazarus, so they say. After life had been breathed into him again, after he had returned from the dead to the land of the living, after Christ had smiled at him softly like the first light of dawn, Lazarus travelled to the shores of our island.

It was the height of summer. The relentless heat parched his throat and that day, as he passed by a lush vineyard which beckoned like an oasis of crystal clear pools of blue, as he wiped the beads of sweat off his forehead, he begged for a drop of water. 'Some grapes,' he gasped. 'Some grapes to quench my thirst.'

The woman who owned the vineyard stood in the shade, looked at this strange man, at his long, grey hair, his old clothes and dusty feet, looked him up and down, up and down, and said in her cool voice: 'This year my vineyard has dried and we have produced no grapes.' Instantly, they say, he cursed her for her lies, cursed with fury at the black, fleshy, juicy bunches hanging from the branches. He cursed her voice, the bitter cruelty he had heard in it, and turned her vineyard into salt water.

It is on the edge of this very lake that you will see the Hala Sultan Tekke of Umm Haram, the revered mosque, the holiest place of pilgrimage for the Moslems in Cyprus. When you go through the ornate gate with its spiral inscriptions in Arabic, the dates in gold, you will find one of the calmest places on the island. Here, they say, is the spot where an aunt of Mohammed died on her travels, fell off a mule and broke her neck. This is where she is buried. Her spirit sometimes walks over these salt waters in the haze of the blinding sun and she whispers: 'I am here. This is my tomb, forever at the edge of salt tears, under the shade of the tall, proud palm trees. Here I am. But oh, how I still wanted to live!'

Why do the flamingoes return year after year? What wisdom pulls them to the same spot where a Christian and a Moslem were both bitterly disappointed? Why do they bring fire with them in the heart of winter and then silently stoop their necks as if searching for answers from the deep sediments, the old earth? The bitter waters mirror them exactly.

Every year, I ask the flamingoes to tell me the answer. They promise: 'Next year, next year,' and all through the summer I look into the skies. Every year they come, and every year their reply is the same: 'Next year, next year,' as they become one big flame, engulf the sky, and extinguish themselves in the distance.

The Cyprus Problem

Two well-known politicians during a live televised debate discuss the Cyprus problem:

'We all realize that part of this island is missing but nobody knows how to put it back.'

'Why do we want to put it back? Is there any need for a part of you that's been missing for 30 odd years to be put back?'

'Do you want to be incomplete, and missing one of your vital organs, e.g. your heart, for the rest of your life?'

'If you have managed to live without your heart for so long, do you really want it back?'

'But if you don't have a heart, doesn't it mean you are technically dead?'

'Technically, yes, technically. But as we lie dead in our grave pretending not to hear anything, the other half is floating away, and that's what the problem is.'

'Let's just cut the crap because what we are basically saying is that we are talking crap because there is no solution to the Cyprus problem. Because there is no solution to the Cyprus problem. Because there is no solution to the Cyprus problem. Because there is no solution to the Cyprus problem.'

'Because nobody has ever found a solution to the Cyprus problem.'

'Yes. Because there is no solution there is no solution there is no solution.'

No-Man's-Land

Yesterday they pulled down the house I was in love with. The derelict house in No-Man's-Land, whose walls came crashing down reluctantly, in slow motion, as if they had been made of a substance stronger than sandstone. For as long as I can remember, perhaps for as long as I have lived, its half-walls had stood still like time on an abandoned clock, grass growing in the cracks, sparrows building nests in the gaps, in the rain, in the sun, the house had stood still.

Whenever I walked past on a humdrum errand in the heart of the city, rushing to get to one place or another before closing time, I would inevitably stop for a short moment and breathe in its lost grandeur, its fading façade, its loneliness.

Yesterday I stood some distance away from the rubble and dust, and imagined one last time the set of the film I would have made here, had I been a director. I resurrected the golden urns which had once decorated its entrance, the Persian carpets which covered wooden floors and hushed footsteps, the colonial etchings which graced its walls, the costumes of its last inhabitants, their final, polite conversations at the long, polished dining table before time engulfed them, sucked them in, ate them. Before this, before now. Then, then.

I tried but, for the first in many months, couldn't. What remained of the set for the film I always directed in my mind with minor alterations, as I walked by, was the tall, stoic palm tree. A tall palm tree, its fringe of leaves swaying above my head in the slight breeze, a tall palm tree in No-Man's-Land.

When you walk the streets of Nicosia, my father used to say, you walk on the wounds of history. The city aches, you can feel it. Walk quietly, walk carefully, walk gently. Can you hear the groans? Can you feel the pulse? And we walked and walked the narrow streets, down the alleys, round corners, and when we reached the Venetian walls, he would put my small hand on the rough stone, cover it with his, and say 'Shhh! Listen to the story on the other side.' I was quite certain when I was young, that my father would never die. That he would live to be ninety or a hundred, that he would teach me, my children, everything he knew.

When I look back over my shoulder at my childhood, it is always autumn. There is always a wind blowing on my face, making me look with my eyes half-shut, at a world half in focus. The cool wind on my face is sharp, dispersing thoughts like dry leaves, like messages on yellow paper, messages I cannot catch or read, they fly away, never land, never rest.

There is no autumn on Mediterranean islands. It is a passing winter, briefly spring, mostly summer. There is no autumn, so I make it up, from what I have read in books, seen in films. I invent this autumn because I do not want the events to take place, as they did, in the heart of a Cypriot summer, in the glaring heat – the heat which makes you frown even in the shade, burns every blade of grass in sight, melts rooftops. Because it seems almost obscene to remember that at my father's funeral I could smell the dead body decomposing in the overheated coffin, the overcrowded church, surrounded by the hundreds of candles, the wilting flowers, mixing with the pungent smell of sweat on our black clothes, an atmosphere as hot as our hot tears. No, no. I have often wished my father had died in an English autumn, that a cool breeze had passed over his face as it went still, his lips parted a fraction, and he let out a contented sigh before passing onto the other side of time, without a single memory of heat, without the slightest discomfort.

My mother sat despondently still, stubbornly quiet. Her face was pale, even paler that humid night under the hospital lights which whitewashed, which purified. She sat still by his side, her dark eyes and her white face dry, staring into space, as if she was watching activities taking place in another world, activities invisible to the rest of us. There was now a strange distance between the living bodies in the hospital ward, the distance created by death, a total blank we now had to face and come to terms with. All I could hear was the sound of my mother's breath when finally these words emerged from her mouth. 'You know,' she said, as if solely addressing the nurse who was efficiently handling the tubes, removing bottles, folding sheets, picking up slippers. 'He never loved anyone. He was incapable of love.'

They were the most painful words I had ever heard. More painful even than the goodbyes I have heard from past lovers, more painful even than the goodbyes I have said in order to let go. At that moment I felt as if something vital to my life was being sucked out of my body, being passed through my chest to be violently exposed in the open air. Opposite me, on the other side of the bed, stood another woman, her eyes swollen with weeping. How ugly she looked, and yet how gentle her eyes were, how soft her cheeks when wet with tears. Through my falling tears I caught glimpses in double vision of the young man next to her. He must have thought me terribly ugly too, the way I scrunched the tissues up in my hands, like wet pink hearts, blue hearts, the way I inelegantly let them fall into the small bin full of the cotton wool and elastoplast, injections which may have held traces of my father's body hair, his skin, his blood.

We were the four people who witnessed my father's death. His wife, her son. My mother, me.

In my early student days in England I was desperately lonely. I lived on the first floor of a student residence of the University, a small room overlooking the quadrangle with its lush green, two oak trees and visiting squirrels. I had never seen a squirrel before. Watching them from my window, I became fascinated by the small furry creatures with their shiny little beady eyes, busily scurrying up and down trees carrying on their tail the smell of secrets they had discovered in humans' footsteps.

On either side of my room, behind the walls on my left and right lived two other students, a dark, quiet young Asian man a little older than the rest, who was given to playing a booming music every Saturday and Sunday evening, and a blond girl whose washbasin spluttered loudly early in the morning, regular as clockwork, and woke me up. I later found out she was in her second year of medicine, but with her dangling earrings, lurid make-up and gypsy clothes she looked to me nothing like a potential doctor. Too homesick to notice anything around me, too self-conscious of my accent to talk to anyone, I would politely greet them when we met on the stairs, or waited for each other to cook in the kitchen, or when we crossed each other while walking all the way down the corridor to the bathroom at one end, and the public telephone at the other. I phoned home once or twice, and said in whispered tones, though I was not speaking in English, to my mother at the other end: I want to come back, I hate the food, the weather, the people. It was my first autumn, the autumn term, the English autumn.

It was in that first English autumn, too, that I met John, my first lover, and my first love. I can still smell his skin, as if we were still lying together, as we used too, on the narrow bed, the bed which was really for one student body, not two, the bed made once a week by the cleaner, who would tuck the linen and blankets so tightly under the mattress that it had the austerity of a hospital bed.

A hospital bed. Tonight my father lies lifeless in a hospital bed.

My lips tremble slightly when I remember John sleeping next to me, the way I studied his eyelids when he tumbled into a deep, soft sleep, his mouth slightly open, his lips exhausted from my kisses. It all seems so, so long ago. Now, years later, we sit, a million autumns apart, and my father is dead. My love for him, for them both, is screaming out of my body, into the corridor, the car park, and into the world. And who will be able to find it and bring it back? Who, I ask myself.

Our first night in the bed where John recites a poem, our last night in the same bed. We lie together and I wait for him to say something, anything, but he doesn't say it. He keeps these words inside, the words that are on the tip of his tongue are left unsaid. They must be the most terrible words I have heard, the loudest silence. 'Shhh! Listen to the story on the other side.'

The night my father died, I dreamt of John. I was a student again, sitting in a corner of the library, hunched over titles, reading and not reading, distracted by the sweet smell of the English summer, its long light days, lured by the freedom of daydreaming and covering the margin of my notepad with snippets of poems as they came into my mind, 'breezed in and out of my thoughts', as John would say.

And there they are again, in my dream, a pair of pale blue eyes watching me intently. John's eyes were the blue of lakes. His face wore the intense look of an artist, an actor or writer. What I noticed about him first was not his short ash blond hair, slightly crooked nose or full lips, but only his poet's eyes. In my dream I have the peculiar sensation of finding something precious I lost somewhere long ago. In my dream, John nods his head. 'Yes,' he says, 'Yes. I miss you too. Come and find me. I am in No-Man's-Land.'

Was it autumn, then, or summer, when a non-existent man called No Man moved into a beautiful house abandoned a few hours before? Did he know he would live here for over thirty years in the company of cockroaches, lizards and stray cats? And is it my imagination that even on the stillest summer day, the palm tree seems to be swaying from side to side as if being pulled and pushed by an invisible wind, now from the south, now from the north …?

'It is a journey,' my father used to say. 'Life is a journey. For some it lasts longer than for others.' And where is he now? Is he walking somewhere invisibly towards the end of his journey? Has he finally reached his destination?

Nothing is as it seems, I know that now. For years, my father was my own. I thought we owned him, that he owned us, that we were a family, just the three of us. Yes, we were a family, an unshakable unit, and nothing would ever change that. My father would live to be ninety, or a hundred, and teach me everything he knew.

When I returned that summer, at the end of my first year at university, my father had left my mother for another woman. An amicable decision, they both said. 'Because we had drifted apart …', 'We didn't want to tell you …', 'You had your exams to worry about.'

Suddenly there was no meaning to life. There were no real reasons for anything. I was cold in the middle of summer, I was warm in the middle of winter, I was furious, I was indifferent, I cared, I couldn't care less. It was all a lie. Our life together had been a lie. Everything I had believed in was a lie.

'*He never loved anyone. He was incapable of love.*'

Was it true then? Perhaps. Perhaps there was truth in these words. Perhaps I heard these words from my mother's lips long before my father died. Did he love us, had he ever loved me, why was there so much distance between us now, what had become of our relationship? These were questions which were impossible to answer. I knew that my father now lived with another woman, who had a son of about my age. Did he love them? Did they love him? Every night, these questions kept me awake.

For years, I believed in the passing of seasons. I believed that there must be a summer after spring, and autumn before winter. There had to be clues, hints, changes – even on a Mediterranean island.

All your life, you dream of sunshine, you pray for rain. And suddenly, somebody pulls the carpet from under your feet and you have no idea where you are, somebody cancels all the seasons and you don't know where you stand. You do not know how you will cope. Somebody pulls down the house you were born in, the house you grew up in, the house you were in love with.

The walls come crashing down reluctantly, in slow motion, as if they are made of a substance stronger than sandstone.

Suddenly, someone you once turned to for all your problems turns quiet, and dies. The dead body decomposes in an overheated coffin. You find yourself in an overcrowded church, surrounded by hundreds of candles and wilting flowers, and there is the pungent smell of sweat on your black clothes, an atmosphere as hot as your hot tears. No, no. My father did not die, as I would have wished, in an English autumn. There was no cool breeze passing over his face as it went still, and his lips did not part to let out a contented sigh before he passed onto the other side of time.

There is no autumn on Mediterranean islands, so I make it up. In the same way I make up the stories my father never told me, about life, and love, and all the reasons why.

Afternoon Tea

Mrs So and So having tea with Mrs Such and Such, and their fingernails so long and polished and pearly pink. The china cups clink on saucers, and a musician grandly plays the grand piano raised on a platform in the corner. Old songs, gentle songs while the ladies talk about This, That and the Other. Or the Other, That and This. Different orders, same topics, and the young receptionist balances a pen on her fingers and looks at the clock slowly going tick-tick. Soon, the end of her shift. Soon, home.

At five thirty on the dot, the mask comes off her face. The faultless mask, the May I Help You smile, and the question mark in the lines running from the sides of her nose down to the curves of her lips. Immaculate. She takes it off and hangs it in the staff wardrobe marked TOMORROW.

Mediterranean Blue

Her name is Aphrodite. She is the Goddess of Love.

Sometimes in the crowd gathered round the tourist guide, all listening intently, she finds a pair of eyes squinting in her direction. They are eyes which have no sunshades to hide behind. Brave eyes, she likes that.

And then she speaks to them – only silently, silently, like a little breeze in the heat, cool upon this visiting face, one of so many who come and go, come and go, every day.

Climb up, my friend. Up the hill, follow the footpath lined with anemones, up, up to the site. The white of the ruins against the blue of the sea will dazzle you, it is so strong under the sun, this white. And the blue, it is Mediterranean blue – how can I explain – you are too pale, too new here, oh, but this blue! You must live it, you must breathe it, to understand.

Sometimes in the crowd gathered round the tourist guide, all listening intently, she finds a pair of eyes which want to know more.

Up there, you will find the earth gaping open where they have dug the past. So proudly they announce dates discovered, and chambers unearthed, and show you jewels and vases and skeletons and tell you facts, and facts … But they know nothing. They don't know that they have only scratched the surface with their nails.

My friend, let me tell you. This island has many, many secrets. More than you can see. Yes, hidden secrets of war, of hate, of blood, of pain, everywhere dreams shattered and voices buried. And sometimes where I stand, I feel the pain under my feet, it is so loud, the pain of this land. We forget when or where or who buried it, but it is there below. And many years after, they come and dig and sweat, and dig and sweat; and they find a lot of things – but never the pain.

Nor the love, my friend. This island, you know, we call the Island of Love because I rose from these waves. I whispered the words 'I am Aphrodite' to the sun, and the sun, yes, stroked my body with his rays, and the sea licked my feet as I stepped on the shore. Ah, the blue I was born in is so delicious, and so difficult to describe, and strokes and stings, like love.

Sometimes in the crowd gathered round the tourist guide, all listening intently, Aphrodite finds a pair of eyes which are in love. The eyes look across the sea, the taut blue borrowed from the sky.

Love. It has the power to tear the sea to shreds, I

know. I have stood here and watched it being shred to pieces, or sewn back together by mermaids, again and again. Because minutes, hours, years, centuries are different, but love is the same. Always.

Sometimes in the crowd gathered round the tourist guide, a pair of eyes is not listening. The eyebrows, she notices, come together in a way that is angry. At what – who knows? The sun, the heat, the dust, everything. Back home, the cold, the rain, the crowds, everything. Who knows?

Let the blue balm soothe you, my friend. It is Mediterranean blue. When you see it, remember and forget. Both. Dig and bury. Both. The love and the pain. Both. For this is the archaeological site of Life – and everybody is still digging for the answers.

Her voice becomes one with the ripples. One tourist turns to take a snapshot of Aphrodite's Rock, where she sits smiling.

History

We went to the museum together one day. How romantic.

I met him after work and we had coffee. Then, he said he had to make a sketch of the statue of Aphrodite (the one all the tourists come to look at) for his new painting, and could we go to the museum? That is if you want to, he said, I'm not forcing you or anything.

We went. He didn't force me or anything. I said I couldn't even remember if I'd ever seen that statue in my life. Only in pictures, I said. It was great that she was kind of symbolic, really. Of love, right? No, no he said. Of beauty. And then we nearly had an argument about whether she was the Goddess of Beauty or of Love.

Nearly argued, but not quite, because at that point he picked up his rucksack (I was glad because it was the one I had given him for Christmas. Oh thanks, he had said, I needed one with many pockets inside, how did you know?) and took his sketchpad out and said, Well we can decide later, when we've seen her. Yeah, right, I sneered. Well why not, why not? He always repeated a question when he was annoyed with me. We're people, aren't we? People are allowed to make up their own minds, aren't they? Aren't they? I kind of liked the fact we would get to decide. Beauty or Love.

We walked through the entrance of the museum and all the time I had a hum at the back of my mind of that Bananarama song which said that she was the summit of beauty and love, that Venus was her name and that she's got it, yeah baby, she's got it. I nearly sang him the song, but decided against it because a) I wouldn't want to be thrown out for singing and b) he wouldn't think the lyrics of a 1980s pop song could be taken seriously.

And there she was, in the middle of the room. Beside her all other exhibits faded into insignificance. So white! Totally white, and only half a woman, but she really had stage presence. Much better in still life than in photos, I thought. Although: If I was a kid on a school visit, I might wonder how she had her hair all done, when she had just come out of the water, not a hair out of place. And if I were a teenager from a state school I might wonder how that milky white body and those large hips were supposed to drive men wild.

While he was putting Aphrodite down on paper, I looked at the other exhibits. Not much, really. A couple of smaller statues of men with curly beards. Votaries, they call them. Not really my style. Some vases, pots and jewels from the Neolithic era. And other unearthed treasures. There were a few tourists. Four, five, or six, a couple, and another, and a young woman wearing glasses taking copious notes, standing for ages in front of every exhibit.

One of the tourist women (in her twenties) pointed at something in the displays, and burst out laughing, which made one of the guards give her a funny look, not strict, just funny, because Europeans are different and we know that. I think, in retrospect, that the copious note-taker turned round to look at us. Or just him, perhaps. I can't be sure. And possibly, he looked at her, recognised her from all the lectures we used to go to in room E103 at the University. Had she been there at one of his lectures? Was she an Erasmus student taking an interest in local history? Anything is possible, I know that now.

I looked at the European tourists. There was a time we thought Europeans had a different sense of humour. And other sleeping and drinking habits. But aren't we nearly Europeans? he said to me one day, while we were EU-ing. I mean, he said, isn't Cyprus nearly part of the EU? But does that necessarily make us Europeans? I retorted, thinking that was quite clever of me, because I know deep down, it does not, we are not. Not really.

After the Copenhagen summit euphoria we all thought we had it made. And then we had a look at a newspaper article which said that things would change. And another article in the same newspaper, which said they wouldn't, not really. And we looked at each other and laughed. EU-ing was fun. We did that sometimes in bed. I am Germany, I'd say, and here I come to invade you, you little frog! Ah, but what if I'm Switzerland and I don't really want to play? Then you're a boring old twit, but good enough to eat like your mountains of chocolate. Tonight I'm cold Sweden, and you're my hot Italy. I'm gonna melt you like mozzarella and cover all my euros with you.

All was well. Before Aphrodite. And Tomb 79.

At some point I decided to walk out of that room and go on to the next one. I wandered in and out of the narrow corridors in front of little wooden boxes of displays, without paying much attention, but reading some of the notices. I made notes of the most interesting ones, and thought they would make good titles for paintings at an exhibition: Limestone Snake Coiling Round Cornucopia. Pendants of Picrolite, Chalcedony and Diabase. Bone Tools. Model of Ploughing Scene, 2000BC. Etc. It was getting very warm probably, outside. It felt like it anyway. The guard sometimes looked up at me, but mostly he was intent on polishing his shoes with his eyes. He was sitting on a traditional Cypriot chair. That was cool, I thought. He could be one of the modern-day exhibits, that's how I saw him. I mentally gave him a title, as I walked past: Cypriot Museum Guard On Duty Sitting Uncomfortably on Van Gogh Style Chair or: Dying of Boredom.

I walked out and then up the stairs. And then into the room that was to ruin my day. Or at least, my day out to the museum with the man (I thought) I was in love with. Because (I think) he understood me best of all. He wanted, he once told me, to be a better man because of me. (I saw that in a film once, don't know when. A crook says to his girlfriend: you make me want to be a better person and the girl cries and cries, and it was wonderful at the cinema, because I could cry, too, in the dark. Cinemas are wonderful because you can see and others can't see you. I have cried my eyes out more than once. But the one time he was with me and we went for a drink afterwards, he kept looking at my red eyes and thinking 'Christ! She really has feeling for makebelieve!' I know his thoughts because he told me them later. Much, much later. 'But it wasn't the makebelieve I was crying at,' I said. 'It was because I want to believe that such relationships exist.')

So. I found myself in the room. The big, ugly room at the top of the stairs where I came face to face with two exhibits: Throne and Stool with gilded silver rivets from Salamis Tomb 79. Ivory bed from Salamis Tomb 79. The throne and the stool and the bed of an unknown king … I wanted to sit on those. They looked so fragile, and I was sure if I were to look more closely I would see specks of dust and bits of the earth they had been found in. Really, really deep down underground like a secret throne for the dead, in the earth, and the silver rivets looked so used, not silver in colour but blackening like rotten teeth. I have to admit at this point my stomach turned. And then the bed. The ivory bed. People would sleep on it. How many? Two would fit in, into this ivory deathbed, the frame of a bed, an empty bed, a frame minus canvas. That sick taste came into my mouth. Ridiculous! Should pull myself together … And the smell of the room. Of death.

I had to sit on the van Gogh chair. The guard was all concern. Are you all right? Shall I get some water? No, no my boyfriend. Call my boyfriend. He's with Aphrodite (but of course he can't still possibly be – then – where – ?) I got up, looked into the guard's moustache (I hadn't noticed it before), looked away, then walked away. Said thank you, while walking. Thought perhaps I should find Aphrodite, or should I go to the café across the road and have a coffee and recover, should I wait at the entrance …

Some stories just have to have sad endings. I had that feeling after my visit to Tomb 79 that the day would end badly, if not sadly. That was the point when the guard started talking, his eyes burning through me like coals or something. There is something ludicrous about a museum guard who tries to chat you up in the middle of a room full of exhibits, we are the only two people alive in here, and he says things like What is your boyfriend's name and why has he left such a beautiful girl like you on her own and the colour of your necklace matches your eyes and and and –

I am leaving the room, I think I am running. Yes, it is now very warm. Where the hell is he? Where the hell is he? Is this a nightmare or a bad joke? Is he in cahoots with the moustachoed guard to test me or did we at some point decide to play hide and seek? Why do museums have so many corridors and stairs and rooms and where has Aphrodite disappeared to? I have visions of the Erasmus student and my boyfriend having medium-sweet coffee across the road. She must look so clever with her blond hair and blue eyes and a pen poised at the edge of her lips, when she says 'I'm writing an article on the cult of Aphrodite. Actually …,' then she smiles coyly and he realizes she is actually quite pretty, '... the article concentrates on sacred prostitution.' 'Oh, really?' he says, 'I'm painting Aphrodite, and other women. A kind of collage of different women with an emphasis on beauty. So you're a student …'

I finally reach the room where Aphrodite stands in all her naked glory, and there he is, still sketching. In my excitement at returning to something like sanity and safety, I nearly wave, but don't. Because there, in front of one of the glass cases, still taking copious notes, is the girl taking copious notes.

I don't know how long I stand there and look at him, her, Aphrodite. 'Where have you been?' he says, looking up a moment from his sketchbook. Then, noticing the peculiar expression I must have on my face, adds: 'Are you all right?' I tell him I'm not, that I want to leave. He closes his sketchbook (reluctantly?) and puts his hand on my shoulder. 'I'm sorry,' he says, 'I shouldn't have dragged you in here.' Yes, I thought, that was probably the problem. Lovers drag each other here there and everywhere under the pretext of love, take each other to places one of them doesn't really want to be. Perhaps that is what they mean by 'incompatible', and when does it suddenly hit you that you are 'incompatible'? Who realizes it first? What a silly place, a museum, to realize that all is not really all that well. Yeah, baby, you've got it. The summit of beauty. And love. I'm not forcing you or anything.

When do couples fall out of love? When did I stop loving my artist boyfriend? Was it there and then in the Cyprus museum, or was it a few weeks later at the supermarket, or months later when we lay on the beach and he sketched me, or was it never, because we had never, ever actually been in love?

(The guard gives me the glass of water, and I leave, saying thank you as I walk away. And still, at that point, I think I am in love with a man who is good, but promises to be better. And who repeats questions when he is annoyed. And I want to tell him: But it wasn't the makebelieve I was crying about. It was because I want to believe that such relationships exist.)

The rest, as they say, is history.

Spoon Sweet

Whenever they came to ask for my hand, I usually showed them my back.

'My hand is mine, mamma,' I would say. 'I don't want any of them to take it.'

'Why? Why?' The exasperated, high-pitched word, always repeated twice, would travel from one kitchen cupboard to the other, as she took out sugar, or salt, or put back a jar or a cup. 'One too tall … the other short … one too young … another too old!' Forks and knives were placed on the table with much vehemence. 'What do you want, huh, what is it you want?'

I knew just one thing. I wanted my married life to be as delicious as spoon sweet. 'Spoon sweet?' she laughed, '*Glyko tou koutaliou*? Which flavour then? Walnut, peach or cherry? Home-made or from the supermarket?' And her voice was anything but sweet.

Sometimes, though, she would change her tone when she spoke to me. Even my father looked up from the newspaper from time to time, to make sure it really was his wife speaking, and not an actress in a Greek tragedy on television. It seemed to me then that her voice was steeped in enormous amounts of syrup, positively dripping with honey. 'Marigo,' (every syllable a honey drop) 'it is time for you. Think. Over twenty-five and not yet married. Think.'

I thought. Not married to her best friend's son, who would smack his lips at the mention of the word 'dowry'. Not married to the accountant (Chartered, studied in England) who wanted a healthy wife. Not married. When I looked in the mirror I imagined a bride – not a solemn, white-faced, taffeta-feathered dove, but a colourful parrot, so pretty with its lustrous green, red, yellow feathers. Not in a cage, but out among lush leaves. That was what I wanted.

When I met Kostas, I told him about my spoon sweet dream. Spoon sweets, my grandmother made them. I grew up with those big jars on our windowsills, fascinated by the fruit floating in thick syrup. How they preserved their essence, while becoming something else! A fruit, a sweet, two in one. That, I said to Kostas, is one true marriage.

I explained that I couldn't possibly live in bitterness. There was too much of that already on the island, didn't he agree? As for the wedding, well … I imagined vivid colour, all the guests dressed in reds and yellows and greens, and instead of champagne, sherbet, lots of it, for everyone to drink. All around, on every plate, sticky sweets with pistachio nuts; crunchy deep-fried balls of dough soaked in rosewater, and all kinds of sugar and cream and cinnamon filled pastries, almond daktyla dripping of orange blossom syrup, and …

Kostas was looking at me in a way that made me stop. I really had gone too far, too soon. And now, it was too late. I perfectly understood that look. I had seen it so often on my mother's face, that mixture of frustrated incomprehension and puzzled pity.

But then the unexpected happened. 'Do you think,' he asked, 'do you think …' (and he said this in a very matter-of-fact tone) 'that the same would apply to the honeymoon?'

The words 'honey' and 'moon' had never held so much meaning for me as they did at that moment, coming as they did, married like bride and groom, out of Kostas' mouth. A moon of honey, yes, I liked that. A honey-filled moon, yes. It was the right question, at the right time.

I gave him my hand to hold. And, eventually, to keep.

The Secret

'What do you think of my hair?' asks Niki.
Her husband looks up from the newspaper
and gives a nod. 'It's nice.'

'Yes, but is it really nice?' she insists, because
she is in the mood for insisting.

Usually, men are not the best judge. She would
rather ask her friend Angela, but Angela is away for
the weekend. Gone to Athens, to see a big show.
And to shop.

'I told you it's nice,' he says while his eyes scan
the football results. Then he does something he
doesn't do very often. He looks up at her again.
Now she is confused. Usually he talks to her with
his eyes on the newspaper, especially on a Saturday,
especially when she's just been to the hairdresser's.
Now, she is confused, because he is looking at her.
Something is wrong with her hair, she can feel it,
and she takes a surreptitious glance at the mirror
behind him, to make sure that her hair is exactly the
way it was when she left the hairdresser's. And he
regrets taking a better look because, now that he

thinks about it, he doesn't like what she's done to her hair.

Niki waits, and a blush creeps into her pale cheeks.

'It makes you look cheap,' is what he wants to say. He considers a better way of putting it. 'It's, it's … Wasn't it better before?' he dares. And then reflects on whether there will ever be peace and quiet in this living room ever again.

'No. No. This is the latest fashion. Streaks of different shades of red. Angela had it done exactly like this last week.'

Angela. Right. Of course, he thinks. I might have known.

Eyes back on the newspaper. Niki breathes a sigh of relief. There is nothing wrong with her hair after all.

In an album of wedding photos, years ago, Niki's hair is brown, its natural colour. Once upon a time there was a wedding, her friends say on their occasional visits, and do you remember Niki's dress? And Niki, what was that secret smile on your face? Tell us, tell us.

And Niki will have to think long and hard, because she has actually forgotten the secret, if there ever was one. So she takes them through the photos once again. Look at Marios' face! And what were we wearing, all that pink taffeta! Oh, look at his mother, God rest her soul. And loooook at you over here Angelaaaaaaaaaa! We looked so much older than twenty-five! Oh, and here I am with the secret smile.

It's still a secret.

Veronica Ha Ha Ha

I wonder what happened to Veronica. After she died, I mean. Is it true, for instance, that worms ate into her? And that her hair grew a little bit after the 12th of May 1990?

Veronica laughed a lot. A lot. There was no telling when Veronica would laugh next, at what, or why. But nobody cared much, because she was happy, pretty, young. 'What are you laughing at, Veronica?' we would ask. And she would laugh even more, a tinkle, tinkle laugh and her eyes all wrinkle, wrinkle at the edges, and her teeth like pearls, and her blonde head thrown back.

Most boys and the art teacher fancied her. It was almost as if laughter spun webs round the spiders of silence in people's hearts. I could see the effect it had on men, a kind of Pied Piper of laughter.

The art teacher thought Veronica was brilliant at art. Because she laughed so much, her still-lifes were 'Very good, Veronica. Very good indeed.' And Veronica would laugh. Very, very Onica. Veronique. Nique. Nica.

Then she started dating boys, and her laughter

was heard at the cinema, keeping time with the bass music at the discos, at the back of cars. Well, she had a good life, my good friend. Short, but sweet. Until she went over the cliff and her laughter was eternally frozen in the depths of the sea. Deep sorrow, deep sea. And I don't know now whether to laugh or cry.

'It is with deep, deep sorrow that we are gathered here to say goodbye to our dear Veronica,' said the Headmaster, 'whose laughter so often filled this hall … and our lives.' There were so many sobs. Especially the art teacher.

'Try it,' said Veronica. And the more I tried to imitate her laughter, the more she laughed. 'Not like that!' she tinkled. 'You need an image, see. Like Marilyn Monroe, like Madonna. Some girls pout their lips. I just laugh, even when I'm sad. Nobody can tell the difference.' So laughter is a mask, I thought. A shiny mask to hide the darkness beneath.

'Will you be able to keep up this laughter?' I asked, thinking we had years ahead.

'Of course!' said Veronica. 'For as long as I live. It's the easiest thing.'

'When did you start laughing?'

'When I was seven, and my father starting abusing me. That's when it started, because it was the saddest, saddest part of my life.'

She wasn't stupid, Veronica. And I suppose I liked her. She showed me a different world, a world where things were possible, easy to get – boys, cars, admiration. Some parents thought she was on drugs, including mine. 'Watch out who you're hanging out with,' said my father. 'You'll end up like her if you're not careful.' He meant like a junkie. I longed to tell him that I didn't want to be like Veronica: I wanted to *be* Veronica.

'The poor girl is mad,' said my mother. 'What do you expect, with a French mother, and a lunatic at that?' Her parents had divorced when she was nine, the year her mother had suffered a breakdown. 'Just keep away from that girl.'

And I studied and studied for my French O-level, but I didn't keep away. I sometimes practised with Veronica's mother, whose hands shook, who never laughed. *Tout ce qui brille n'est pas or.* All that glitters is not gold. She nodded. 'Oui', she said from time to time, looking at her hands, as if explaining the meaning of life to herself: 'Oui, oui, c'est ça.' And only once, she looked at me without seeing me, and announced: 'Oui, et ce n'est pas une hirondelle qui fait le printemps.' I translated the sentence, word for word, for practice: 'Yes, and one swallow doesn't make the spring.' And Veronica laughed. And her mother burst into tears.

'You can have it when I die,' Veronica once told me. 'Like a kind of transplant.'

It was a will. She was leaving me her most prized possession; an idea that kept me awake at nights. Something to lure with, even in a clichéd kind of way, to kill for. So I wished and willed her to die, so that I could inherit her laughter.

If I could rewind the film to the point where it happened, if I could press 'stop' and then start editing, cutting bits out, adding special effects, smoothing life, playing a God who can change the past, I probably would. Yes, our lives would be different, happier for some, sadder for others.

I was sitting at the back of the car. That was my fate. Veronica and Sam were at the front, and Sam was driving, that was their fate. 'I'll come later,' I said. 'I'll get my dad to drive me.' Veronica insisted. 'No, don't be silly, you can come with us.' So I went with them to the meeting place for the open-air art lesson, where we were supposed to get a feel for the sea, the shells, the coast, the light. I say 'went' but what I mean is 'didn't go', because we never made it.

Deux s'amusent, trois s'embêtent was on my mind. Two's company, three's a crowd, so I wasn't really paying much attention. I remember the music, Sam asking Veronica to open the glove compartment to take out his brand-new driving license, and Veronica laughing at the photo, and passing it to me, with her head in between the two front seats, and me looking at the licence without finding it amusing or even interesting.

I looked out of the window at the rocky beach and blinked, I think, for a second.

You blink, and the world changes.

I had wished for the world to change, and it had, and I could never change it back. I am, I was part of it, and the screams wake me up at night. And sometimes I edit the moment.

'Quick,' Veronica says to me, in the edited version. 'Take it. Take my laughter before it dies.' So I take it, since it is bequeathed unto me.

But at first I don't know what to do with it. So I go even quieter for a while, hoping I won't lose it if I open my mouth. Then, the night of the funeral I close my door and stand in front of the mirror. I throw my head back, and to my surprise, it comes out like a tune learnt by heart. Ha ha ha, Veronica. Veronica, ha ha ha. *Rira bien qui rira le dernier.* She who laughs last, laughs best, laughs longest.

Amour fou

I want you to know that the flowers are red
violet yellow that they have a million petals
that there is colour even in our smallest kiss that my
body wants to unmake you from man to boy that
your weight sleeps on top of me in the trembling
night you are beside me and there is a smell of
excitement in the folds of your skin there is
something about you and me which burns my
mouth and my heart I want a far away place to send
the ashes and watch them fly in a gigantic storm I
am drunk on sweet poison and honey I am an Arab
I am a Jew there is perfume in my hair you are the
strangest song I have ever sung you belong to me I
will follow you in the Métro in your dreams in
labyrinths until all the flowers burst open and wine
flows in the streets and trickles down your mouth
you create a new life for me a long silk dress to
tease your lips which stain its white somewhere
there is traffic danger and people who sleep in ice
beds without love mad love is a honeysuckle and a
bee buzzing in the light the beauty of your naked
breath a terrible cry an exclamation which leaves

me and an untamed lust which quivers in its
freedom like a bold scandal or the murder inside a
knife how necessary you make feel when you kill
me with desire and a screech stabs the silence I
want you to know

Ten little Stories of Love and Hate

1. Broken

It was well and truly shattered. A broken vase. A broken marriage.

In people's eyes we were the shattered children, forced to walk barefoot on splinters of adult glass. As if it was our fault, as if we had broken it playing football or doing handstands in the living room. We weren't quite sure when or how it had happened. Had it fallen and broken while mother was dusting? Or had father knocked it over like an ashtray, while watching the news on television? We weren't sure why our life was suddenly and irreparably broken.

In my eyes I glued it back together like a photograph pieced together after it had been ripped. But the glued bits showed, always. 'I'm sorry,' said my father. 'I'm sorry' as if it was all his fault. When I looked in my mother's diary, she had written: 'You have broken my heart. And as for the children, you have broken their lives.'

2. Magnets

They played the magnetic poetry game. *You are the love of my life* he wrote on the fridge one day, with the magnets they had bought at an art gallery in Europe. Every so often, words would appear, be juggled, moved, go missing like teeth on a child's smiling face.

They left each other messages, but neither of them being particularly gifted in poetry, they would sometimes be mundane. They laughed when the words changed lines or made no sense.

One day it read:
You are love
my life
of
the

Another day:
the life love you are
of my

Gradually, quietly, the words disappeared. And one day, he left.

There were no more games to play, and the fridge door was empty, white, like a hospital bed. She shivered to open it, as if opening it would pour out into her kitchen all the despair in the world.

3. Neighbours

The man upstairs was playing his synthesiser.

I often wondered if he was composing or just playing. Sometimes he would sing. And then a girl's voice would join in. But I could tell it wasn't his wife. Perhaps he was cheating on her with this girl's voice. By joining his voice with this girl's, he was cheating on his middle-aged wife.

'We make beautiful music together,' he would say, perhaps.

Or perhaps it was a surprise in the making.

One day he would say to his wife, on their anniversary: 'This is the song I've been composing for you while you've been working at the supermarket.' It would be romantic, a song for his dumpy wife, who had given him two children. She'd never know that when he sang it, he always remembered the girl's eyes.

'This is what love is, sometimes,' I thought. 'Cheating. Or a surprise.'

4. X-Ray

That X-Ray summed up her life: a tumour, purposeless, growing, fat and ugly, the way she saw her life. She knew it (whatever 'it' was) multiplied per second, like somebody's suicidal thoughts: spreading, getting everywhere, pumping her up with death. As she waited, her stomach turned, and she waited. And still hoped.

'Malignant', he said. 'I'm sorry.'

'Life is such a bitch,' she said. And then the tears came. 'I want to live.'

She repeated it, in case he hadn't heard: 'But I want to live.'

5. Dismissed

Hands went up, but most of the answers were (dead) wrong. Never mind. This classroom. These books. These exams. They are not really you, kids. I said: 'There is a real world out there. Live.'

A constant droning (criticisms, threats) buzzed around, to and from the Queen-bloody-Bee's office.

On my way out I thought I heard: 'We'll miss you, Miss.'

6. Fortune-Teller

'Wanna hear your future?' asked the fortune-teller.

She spoke for hours, and I listened. Bunked off work. Why not? Listen, she's made a fortune doing this. So might I.

Tonight I'll put on make-up, wear rings and bangles, and practise: 'Tomorrow gets better.' I'll repeat it, like a mantra.

7. The Beautiful House

It was a beautiful house when they bought it. Alan said he loved her and would never leave her. A few years later, Alan had left, the house was ugly and full of ghosts, and she thought she heard the neighbours sniggering at her unkempt hair and wild garden.

8. The English Alphabet

a. b. c. d … I was teaching the little Lebanese boy the English alphabet. … i. j. k. l … He wanted to drink water. m. n. o. p … He didn't want to write any more … u. v. w … And why was it all from left to right? x. y. zzzzzzzzzzzzz

9. The Moon

I was having breakfast when I saw the moon. Then I remembered I was in love.

10. The Dog

The dog smiled at Abigail, and Abigail smiled back.

Papers

'Papers?' said the tall, handsome man. It took me a second to realize it wasn't a question. It was an order. Perhaps he wasn't handsome, perhaps I'm making it up. I rummaged in the purse strung round my waist to keep the coins in, I took the Kipling rucksack off my back, the rucksack with the hole in one of its pockets, the one I had found in a rubbish bin in the streets of the city. I pretended I had the papers and lost them, or lost them without ever having had them.

'Papers,' he insisted.

All the coins rolled out of the purse and fell on the floor, all of them, the wristbands I make and try to sell, two for a euro, to strange white people in cafés who tell me thank you, no thank you, and shoo me away with their smiles.

'I don't have papers,' I said, and my voice shook. 'But look at my eyes. All of my history. Look at my eyes. Two for a euro. Two for a euro.' I looked straight at him, and hoped.

I don't know what I'm doing in this country away from home. Living, making a living, working, not living, not really working, what shall I call it, how can I put it, why am I here. When he asked me for my papers, I should have run. Run to the sea which brought me here, and then swum away from this island, swum to God-knows-where. Floating in the sea feels good, I've tried that before, nearly drowned when the boat nearly sank and we had to rely on the salt in the sea to keep us afloat, it felt good to be alive, just me and the sea. If someone could teach me how to empty my head of of all my memories, how do you do that, can you think of something other than the past when you are lonely, because that's how people travel, in their heads, when they can't travel any more. That's all I can do, travel in my head.

And they always ask me for papers. To show them who I am, to prove my existence, to give them my date and place of birth, so that they are sure I now exist here, though I once existed in another country. I ran away once and now I want to run back. And every night I dream I am drowning. I dream I am an old man and I'm drowning, drowning and there's no hope of being saved, no one, no one ... I wake up and my face is wet with sea, with sweat, with tears.

Life of an Amoeba

Out of the blue last night, I remembered Mr Green. Mr Green, of all names! Mr Paul Green (B.Sc., Dip.Ed.), Mr Green with his corduroy trousers and his blue shirts, Mr Blue Brown and Green, Mr Earth colours to match his eyes. Karma Chameleon Mr Green, who cared for the environment, who adopted a whale, whose whole face smiled if you asked him about anything to do with recycling.

I remembered my biology book and how I used to doodle in the margins of all the pages and there are just four words which have stuck in my mind: condensation, chlorophyll, gravity and amoeba. That could be five or six words, if you include Human Reproduction.

So nothing really happens when you're sixteen, and books don't teach you anything until you grow up and things start happening, and you learn for yourself. Let's face it, who cares at sixteen when Mr Green tells you things about leaves and oxygen, and why we fly in space and not on earth, and how an amoeba fills its days and nights, crawling all over the floor like a drunkard and a blob. Of course nobody knows for sure if an amoeba enjoys its existence. It doesn't even have sex, except with itself. And I remember doodling AND A LITTLE BIT OF CHLOROPHYLL TO MAKE YOU BREATHE. An advert for good lungs – breathe in – breathe out –

Life is full of cycles, you always return to the beginning. Three or four years after leaving school, four or five years after he had retired, I bumped into Mr Green at a bus stop downtown.

'Mr Green!' I called out, genuinely pleased to see him. 'Is that you? Do you remember me? How are you?' He looked awful, paler than I remembered him, paler and thinner, his eyes still that blue of lakes, his hair gone white, white, white, and his skin so colourless, as if it wasn't really there at all.

'I wish you'd asked me so many questions when I was your teacher,' he said, and smiled, that smile of long ago, the smile of genuine kindness. I wanted to cry there and then, because he was smiling his 'Everything will be all right' smile. 'Of course I remember you,' he continued. 'You were a dreamer, never a scientist.'

My heart was now beating very fast, and I hoped the bus would never come. I wished that I could impress Mr Green by telling him I had become an astronaut, I was a member of Greenpeace, I had discovered a way to make the hole in the Ozone Layer smaller, I had given birth to triplets, I –

'And what have you done with your life?' he asked, as if reading my thoughts, but his lake-blue eyes were not unkind.

Before I could open my mouth to let out a sound, before I could think of anything remotely interesting or important to say, his bus came, and he got on, with a small wave of his hand, and so disappeared forever from my life. Mr Green, Mr Green, Mr Blue Brown and Green disappeared on bus number 43, and there was nothing I could do about it. I didn't even get a chance to say a proper goodbye.

What have I done with my life? Good question, Mr Green. I have been learning facts. The facts of life. And life sucks Mr Green, it is not all blue and green. Even tigers yawn out of boredom, and when they're licking the blood off their claws they are probably thinking that life sucks. Always a dreamer, never a scientist. Yeah. You know what? I am a little amoeba and I have a pseudolife and pseudofriends and a pseudohusband and we have pseudosex and I can't even conceive. Oh, Mr Green, please come back and smile that 'Everything will be all right' smile and I will regurgitate some facts I ought to have learnt from you. All about chlorophyll and the life of the amoeba and everything one needs to know about asexual reproduction. You will be pleased with me, Mr Green. I know you will.

If dried leaves are powdered and digested with

ethanol, after concentration of the solvent, one obtains 'crystalline' chlorophyll.

Asexual reproduction does NOT require fertilization. Asexual reproduction is usually faster than sexual. The new organisms are genetically identical to their parents.

Unicellular protists are able to change their shape constantly.

The amoeba forms pseudopods (false feet) with which it flows over a surface.

And then, Mr Green, when you have patiently listened to all this, perhaps you will tell me what to do about my own life, which doesn't really know where

　　　it's

　　　　　going …

Curtains

'What did you say?'
'What did you say?'

The stress on the word is very important when you're asking a question at the most crucial point in your life. I don't know which 'what' it was I said. When someone's leaving you, you don't really hear what it sounds like. It only feels as if parts of your heart are in your mouth. And your eyes take in his one or two grey hairs for the first time and the chest hairs and the checked shirt and the jeans and the suede shoes. And you wonder if you ever loved this man, who is going, going, gone.

And you wonder why you're wearing white on this day of all, like a silly bride, and is it summer or winter? You feel as if you will throw up part of your heart or your head will explode while you ask him 'What?' when he says 'I'm leaving you'. And you had thought that it had been all right. As safe, as easy as choosing the colour of curtains.

The curtain flaps and you remember the colour you chose together, that elusive colour flapping inside your head, a trapped bird, like you now, like now you. So you watch the man leave.

(Why? What went wrong? you thought later. And the curtains flapped in time with the words: What went wrong? Questions left hanging like curtains.)

And now that I think about it: why 'you'? Swap to 'I' while telling this story, because it is your story and no one else's.

I go into a shop choosing sofas, big or small. 'What size is your flat? What colours?' asks the assistant, a man. I think he should be helping his girlfriend, not customers, choose furniture. As if he were invading my privacy, as if he cares only about showing me samples to watch me suffer or count the lack of wedding rings on my fingers. 'I'm getting married next week,' I say, stroking the velours blue and beige 'Louis XIV' style armchair.

'Would you like a catalogue to show your fiancé?' he asks.

'Yes, thanks,' I reply.

'And a range of colours. You can order them to match. Curtains.'

'Thank you so much. May I sit on the biggest sofa?' The biggest one, for the biggest loneliness, the biggest let-down.

'Please feel free.'

Free? And then a sudden thought comes to me. The man looks endearing enough. Sweet, twenty-four, maximum. Probably just dropped out of college, where he probably jilted a girlfriend and moved to another town and now he's making a living making me choose. Choose what? Choose a space-filler, the cushiest, most expensive space-filler.

'May I ...?'

'Certainly.'

I sit down testing the sponge. I put my head back, grab the armrests, stretch my legs, close my eyes.

The young college dropout is still smiling, but there is something frozen in that smile, like a bird's eyes, like a monkey's grin. I take off my sandals and step on.

'May I?'

'Excuse me?'

'May I? My fiancé's an acrobat.'

The eyebrows that shoot up don't really become a young man. A college dropout should not be shocked at anything.

So, up and down, I jump. Up and down. Like life.

'Thank you,' I say. 'I'd like to invite you to my wedding. Which college were you at?'

'What?' he asks.

Some progress here. Not 'Excuse me?' or 'Pardon?' but 'What?' And the sofa's velours lips turn up into a smile. Like Dalí's 'Mae West'.

Goodbyes

How pathetic I must look. Like those children I once saw at the airport, clinging to their father's legs, screaming their heads off, Don't go, DON'T GO DADDY! Don't!

At least I'm not screaming. At least I'm not crying. At least I'm not even saying anything. 'Say something,' I hear you say. What shall I tell you, you bastard? What do you want to hear? And which language shall I say it in? How do you say auf Wiedersehen, with the dignity of a film star when you really feel like a piece of cloth, perhaps a dish cloth – a what-do-you-call-it- 'tea towel'– as dignified as a tea towel with a Princess Diana head on it, so pretty, so young, so glamorous and oh, so pathetic. Well, I suppose this … Well, I think this is … Well … That's right, kiss the air next to my cheeks, like the coward that you are, all you can do is kiss the air. Go fuck your fucking wife.

(The woman standing in that office saying goodbye is not really me, no, not really. It's me in a past life, a younger person, not yet complete. 'Say something.' Did I say anything? Did I say it in

English? Au revoir? Auf Wiedersehen? What do they say in films? I don't recognise myself. Blonde, and I'm smoking a cigarette, and instead of speaking, I blow smoke all over the place, curls and curls of smoke, I must stop smoking altogether, bad for you, yes, so bad. As bad as eating yourself up with goodbyes you don't really want to say. 'Say something.')

You look so pathetic, I don't even know what I ever saw in you. The eyes of a dog, pretending to be faithful. The lips of a frog. Frog prince. The nose of an eagle, bigger than your face. Jet black hair, some turning grey. I should have counted them. A white shirt with an ink stain on it, an old tie I've seen at least ten times. Small hands, as small as mine. Khaki trousers (yes, who wears khaki these days, for Christ's sake) no sense of colour or style, are you colourblind or just blind or blinkered or all of the above? 'Say something.' What shall I say? What did I see in you, what did you see in me?

(In a beautifully made black and white film, I would have blonde hair and luscious lips, I would be wiping my tears with a white hankie, my eyelashes would be wet and I would be saying auf Wiedersehen, au revoir, as easily and gracefully as holding a cigarette, 'Goodbye, my darling, goodbye, until we see … each other … again,' with all that pretty punctuation, with all those heart-rending pauses, my luscious lips trembling slightly …)

In the real world I do none of the above. In fact, I do nothing, say nothing, look dark and skinny, there are no tears, my lips do not tremble. I just get up. And go.

(Oh look, I can write it now. What I should have said: Au revoir, auf Wiedersehen, goodbye, my darling. May we never see each other again.)

Lemons

London, 12 May

Dear Larry,

I looked for you yesterday. Inside a lemon. I pressed it to my face, whiffed it, rolled it in my hands. A whole lemon, but you were nowhere to be seen. Much against my wishes (for I still love you, Larry, somewhere in the loops of my memory), I took a knife and cut it into two. Division is so bitter, as you know. I resisted the temptation to squeeze the one half, your half, and taste the juice, the yellow potion of Larry love – sharp and quenching, full of zest, demanding attention of all one's senses. (I have not forgotten, Larry.)

And if you go to Kyrenia
Don't go into the walls

One look from you made me a woman – Gypsy, Alexandrian, Jewess. You spoke those words as an identity, caressing them like no-one before you or after you. After you. During you. That's the part I like best. During you. When you wrote and I read and I basked in your attention and the sun was shining, a much healthier sunshine than today.

Today I am cold, even though the sun is out. (Don't you find, Larry, that the sun anywhere else in the world is a pale copy of the Ionian original?) You see, I haven't forgotten.

And if you go into the wall
Don't stay long.

'Come, I will tell you a story. About a souk, a labyrinth of spices. Follow me, Larry, or you will be lost. I know the way. And if we ever come to the walls ... we must ... turn back.' Yes, I was a good story-teller. I was happy. Happy on our walks over the hills. Happy in the sea, dipping myself in that so intense, serene blue. 'Will I come out blue?' I laughed, and you scribbled it in your notebook. I often watched your hands writing, your face reading.

Up and down those waves of words, up and down, the surface of the sea so calm, your eyes so blue and your sentences so stormy. I was afraid (yes, I admit) that one of those waves would one day slap me. Why did I anticipate turbulent waters? That summer I did not see a single rough sea. Why, then, was there a certain noise (how can I define it? a hiss, almost) in my ears, at the back of my mind, reminding me so much of waves dying on the shore? While your waves were being born, Larry, I could hear their death.

And if you stay long
Don't get married

We didn't turn back (turmeric, ginger, nutmeg, chilli, walls, barriers, silence, in that order) and got married too soon. Ripples, ripples, waves, waves. Never again a calm day. Jealousy, doubt, anger churning away ('Don't smile at strangers in that gypsy way', 'Don't look at women with sex in your eyes') in the deep, blue blue.

I remember once after our marriage we made love on the beach, rolling in broad daylit sand (and crushing the dying ripples with our weight), our hair salt-stained and crispy, our lips raw. You were silent afterwards, Larry. After love, there was always no strength in your voice and no loudness in your opinions.

And I was glad that you had no energy left in you, that I had sucked it all, that our roles were for once reversed. That I had shrunk and shrivelled you like grass in the Ionian summer, dried you like the tang of salt in my mouth. That I was the fiery gypsy you married and not the sad woman you paled me into. But I was deluding myself. I think I was sad that day, that moment when our daughter was conceived. And then the slap came. The wave hit me and then that noise. Hissssssssssssssssss...

And if you get married
Don't have children!

How is my sweet child who was born too soon, too late? Too soon for me to love her, too late into the hiss at the back of my mind. Give her my love.

No, my sane caresses. Tell her she has an insane mother who loves her bitterly. No, a bitter mother who loves her insanely. I'm not sure which. You decide.

Your better, bitter half
E.

London, 13 May
Dear Larry,

They are looking after me very well. I think I will soon be able to leave. I have a nice room, quite spacious, with a window overlooking some apple trees. Don't laugh – I often sit here and imagine the apples to be lemons. How is your book coming along?

Love,
E.

Fictional letters addressed to Lawrence Durrell, author of *Bitter Lemons*, from his second wife Eve Cohen, who had a mental breakdown sometime during their marriage. The passages in italics are lyrics of a song quoted in *Bitter Lemons*.

The Book

Three days after she died, he went to the bookshelf in the living room and picked out a book. A red and gold hard cover he had never seen before, covering her much-loved black and white pages. It could have been any book, it was just any book, but her hands had touched it, her eyes had read it. Her lips had smiled with satisfaction after she had bought it, carried the paper bag home, and opened it slowly to savour the pleasure, to press it against her face and smell the pages, to look at the front cover and then read the back cover, before opening it at page one.

He started to read. He tried to concentrate, and read the story of a beautiful Russian princess and the tales she told a bear on a Midsummer's night, the story of a Hindu goddess and her exquisite gold-coloured nails which scratched at the sky to find the sun and the moon, and the fable of a little pink English fairy with skinny legs who laughed and ran on every page, wait till you find me, ha ha ha, wait till you catch me, and she ran in between the trees in the forest of words on every page, and he wept.

Without really knowing why, without really caring why, without any tears, love and regret gushed out, love and regret, and anger and pain and sorrow. You arrange your life, he thought, and sigh with contentment. Then, one day, you open a book, read its stories, and sigh with regret. This book, he thought, was never meant to be read this way, oh no, not this book, not like this.

He remembered a long time ago, when they had the baby. She cried all the time, woke them every night, tore them away from their sweetest dreams. As if she was a little sleep-destroyer sent from another planet. I will not let you, she would bawl, no, no, no, I won't. I have instructions not to allow you to fall asleep! Where was that adamant little creature now, he smiled. Grown up, quiet, and still, probably silently grieving somewhere else, in another house, on another street. I ought to have read these stories to my wife back then, he thought, as her eyelids opened and closed and opened, with early morning sleep fluttering around them. It was now twenty or thirty years too late. He had opened the book too late.

He touched the red cover. Gold sunflowers. A title. A name. Covering the words and protecting them, letting them sleep. It was so late now. Should he leave the book lying next to him on the sofa, or put it back on its shelf, on the hard dark wood which was gathering dust? He did not know what the time was, he had been reading and thinking for so long that he could see the gold outside, the gold of dawn. She would never see it.

She had once tried to learn German. Had tried to read German poetry. Once.

Once upon a time. What he remembered was just like snippets of a story which were flying around the living room, pieces of paper where parts of a story were written: a beginning, a middle, and an unexpected end. Who had written the story, and when? He snatched at them and read what he could see in the dark. Once, once upon a time, an eccentric friend had read their palms for fun. A very short lifeline, she had said to him, as opposed to his wife's very long one. And they had all laughed. Which hand had that friend looked at, which line, he wondered now, and wasn't there a book somewhere, a 'Teach Yourself' book his wife had bought, all about reading the secrets in other people's palms? He sat for a long time like a beggar, with his hands resting on his knees, looking at his empty palms, without actually seeing anything.

So here he was, alone with his thoughts and memories, alone with a book of imaginary tales a German woman had written, an American woman had translated, which his wife had bought and read, he was not sure when. She read a lot, he knew that, but when. Where. He wished he could picture her now in a corner of the living room, reading a book.

Had he ever watched her? Had he ever seen her turning the pages? He had always been far too active for that. Far too busy for sitting still for too long. She would discuss books effortlessly, recommend titles, would ask him if he had read such and such, did he like it, what did he like about it. She always had an opinion, always had time for opinions. I read and re-read the ending, she once told him. I read the last page three or four times.

I read the last page three or four times, and was sorry it had ended. That the back cover had put an end to their lives. I wanted it to go on and on. What do you think about that?

What did he think about that?

And this time he wept uncontrollably.

A Man of Principle

The lift, he assumes, will not be looked at till Monday. Possibly not even Tuesday. Wednesday, perhaps. And he will have to put up with it, like that toothache inside his swollen cheek, about two months ago. Not till Monday, the irritating female voice had told him. The doctor won't be able to see you till Monday. He had suffered all weekend, only to be told at 9:30 on Monday morning that the tooth needed to be extracted; that long wait, only to be reminded that he was getting old beyond repair.

Today's gaping, out-of-order lift reminds him of his mouth at the dentist's, waiting to be looked at, sad, half-open; then – a mirror to reflect all kinds of dirty comings and goings. It will stay open all weekend like a mouth in pain, he thinks, and a mirror inside, for me to see my angry face as I walk past it to get to the stairs. Next time they come round to collect the monthly community charges, I will refuse to pay, refuse point blank. It's a matter of principle.

Mr Haroutune belongs to a generation of men with principles. His all-year-round dark clothes, near-white hair, his horn-rimmed glasses, his slightly hunched back, his silent demeanour, his unsmiling face tell you that he does not want to be disturbed, it's a matter of principle, and all you should know about him is his name. Nothing more, nothing less. And he doesn't really want to know you. Not if he can help it.

OUT OF ORDER. Somebody's untidy scrawl, a piece of paper stuck carelessly on the wall. On your right hand side as you enter the building. Three words stating the obvious. A waste of three words. Words which any of these wretched children playing in the streets could snatch and throw on the floor, along with the wrappers of their crisps, thinks Mr Haroutune.

He swears, as he goes up the stairs, a grey figure, to the first landing. In his right hand he is carrying a green plastic bag, through which a carton of milk is discernible. Light Milk. 0% Fat Milk, but he is Out Of Breath. His knees hurt and his feet shuffle slightly as he continues his slow ascent. He considers the bicycle tyre stains on the walls (those bloody children!), like snake skin ripped and stuck on the walls for decoration. Like all the rubbish you see in art galleries these days. He looks at the names and numbers on people's doors. S. Christou. Mr and Mrs Kyriakos Stylianides. 303, 304 ... 401, 402 ...

One more flight, and when he looks down from the landing in front of Flat 501, the entrance has the width of a medium-sized refrigerator, and the letterboxes the size of small paperbacks.

In the letterbox of H. Darakdjian, there is a letter addressed to a Mr Harout Darakdjian from a K. Darakdjian, Sydney, Australia. He has not seen it yet.

Haroutune Darakdjian reaches the top of the stairs, and takes the key out of his pocket. He goes in, and promptly and gratefully shuts the world out. In the privacy of his home, things that have been annoying him lately buzz around him like mosquitoes. That wretched child has started walking. And twice he's been on the balcony with that stupid woman after him, No!!! No!!! Demetri mou, come back! Not on the balcony!! practically in his ear while he's been watering my plants. At least now, soon, hopefully, he thinks, there won't be a pram to squeeze into the lift, pushing me into a corner, forcing me to look down while the woman acknowledges me, talks to her child and looks at her hair in the mirror, all three practically at the same time. And then when we reach the fifth floor, I help her get the pram out because it's the only way I can get rid of her – them – as fast as possible.

Then, the parrots. The ones in front of the shop across the road. Yesterday there were still the two of them. Today there is only one. A subdued one. Alone now in the cage. Healthy but dead, and the other one: dead but free. No squabbling: a quiet, an unnatural silence.

Mr Haroutune thinks of his wife. The parrot absent from the cage

He doesn't know it yet, but in his letterbox there is a letter from Kevork. Written in English, not Armenian. Dear Dad. (When did he ever call him Dad? When was the last time he had written? When had he last seen his son?) Lisa and I are having problems – have been having problems for some time now …

Haroutune Darakdjian thinks of his wife before falling into a deep sleep, before being shaken awake by the nightmare. A small child, barely 10-12 months old, climbs over the balcony railings and ends up lying on the ground below in a pool of blood, and then as Haroutune is walking up to the entrance with the newspaper in his hand, he sees the baby is still alive and has an immaculate face, not destroyed in the impact, and it is looking at him, but not crying. Haroutune gets down on his knees and strokes its little head, which then starts to bleed, and the face that looks back at him this time is not the neighbour's son, the little boy, but Haroutune's own son, Kevork, baby Kevork. 40 years ago Kevork.

Every evening, Mr Haroutune takes his photos out of the cupboard in the corridor and looks admiringly, nostalgically, sometimes, critically (I should have used better focus there. The sheep is slightly out of focus), even with his weakening eyes he can see the faults, and then the beauties: Kyrenia, the harbour. Bellapaix, Famagusta.

This morning he came across one of his photographs that had been used to illustrate a magazine article, but nowhere was there a credit to him for his photograph. No credits! He will write to them, it's a matter of principle.

The nightmare wakes him up. In a cold sweat, he thinks, for no apparent reason, of the invasion. Of the situation now. He puts his slippers on and goes out onto the balcony. What is happening? All building, building, and all for what? For the Turks to come and take it all? In this wretched half-city, this mutilated city where the Halt signs have given his heart an angry beat for the past 28 years.

He rents the flat he is in now, but pre-1963 he had been rich, a landowner, a good photographer. The best, some said, but he was a realist and knew his shortcomings.

Siranoush would go on and on, about the shop. If. If. If we hadn't built on that side, if, if , if … No use crying over spilt milk, he would tell her. And had even persuaded himself to believe it. But tonight … He agrees with her. All the Ifs come to him on this cold night, and his wife's eyes follow him from the framed photo as he paces. Not for the first time today he thinks of the lonely parrot in the cage. If there hadn't been an invasion. If our son hadn't gone to Australia. If you hadn't died,

Siranoush. I can't sleep, I can't sleep. His throat tightens and the tears start to fall like the first drops of rain.

If.

If.

If.

'You are too young to know anything about the suffering of Jesus, or salvation, or what heaven and hell are,' he says to the bemused Jehovah's Witness (a young man of about twenty-two), 'so I suggest you leave me alone and get back onto your bicycle and go back to where you came from.'

The young man remains politely silent, doesn't press the Down button, but opens the staircase door, one arm still loaded with various pamphlets, and walks down.

'Wretched fools,' mutters Mr Haroutune. 'A boy to teach me about religion! What is the world coming to, what is happening to the world? Am I going mad? Is everyone else? Is this what I have worked all my life for? To live my days in a crazy city, and smile at this smiling fool of a boy who comes knocking at my door to ask if I know about the second coming?'

'There is a mosque practically across the road, you fool, I should have told him,' thinks Haroutune. 'Do you know the difference between a church and a mosque? Between a priest and an imam? You have been in Cyprus for five minutes. You know nothing. Nothing at all.'

Again, he is the photographer in his dark room, his mind. He has captured moments with his camera, and those moments, every moment emerging on paper has become history. History! he considers, because nothing is ever the same again. No two moments are alike.

On the dining room table are the photograph albums he had taken out last night. Strange, he thinks, that I forgot to put them back. It is not like him to forget, but too many things have been on his mind lately; too many thoughts pecking at his mind like hungry little sparrows at scraps of bread … He rarely looks at the photographs during the day, but now he longs for the serenity they give his mind.

He opens the album on top, the red one, at a random page. The Tekke of Umm Haram surrounded by the tranquil blue of the Salt Lake. Next page: The Yeni Djami – the new mosque. He recalls something he once read in a history book. That a Turkish Governor had torn down the walls of an old church which stood in its place, in order to find a treasure. He found nothing, and was beheaded. To lose one's head for nothing! History!

He flicks through the pages. Now in front of him, in all its glory, The Gymnasium at Salamis, where St Paul and St Barnabas proclaimed the word of God … (does the little Jehovah's Witness know that?), then:

Portrait of a Young Peasant Girl ... (how old is she now, how many lines on her face, he wonders) ... One more, he thinks, and looks admiringly at The Potter at Work, one of his favourite moments captured in black and white. *Memento vivere*, he thinks. Or is it *Memento mori*? remembering his school Latin. Latin. That beautiful, stone dead language. That language of the angels who sometimes sing in the silence with the voices of church bells. *Memento mori*. Inevitably. Remember you are to die.

In the flat, time stands still. Outside, traffic, life, the world. He sits, his shoulders sagging, bending his entire being over this single photograph in the spotlight of a single desk lamp as if it is the last photograph he ever captured on film before the present overtook the past, before things changed, before he knew they were changing. Sometimes you stand at the edge of the sea and you think time is coming towards you and somewhere near the distant horizon, is the future. And one day you realize you are closer to the future than you have ever been, that soon, one day, there will be no horizon visible.

The Potter at Work. He still remembers the potter – probably dead now – and the water pot so lovingly coming into being, the clay clinging to his hands, probably long smashed to pieces and being blown about in the air for twenty, thirty, forty years. Unto dust you will return. Both dead, both dust.

'Haroutune! What a surprise! Where have you been hiding you old fool? Sit, sit – he pulls up a chair – I will order a coffee.'

Mr Haroutune is in the shop of his lifelong friend Hagop Keshishian, Jeweller. No two men could be more different, but they are friends. Their friendship has lasted a lifetime, a lifetime even minus their married life, as they have known each other since school. Haroutune, older by seven years, now looks at his friend and feels his entire being relax a little. As the other man talks (for he never stops talking), he is more at home in this little Aladdin's cave than he has been, anywhere, for a long time.

He breathes in the warm comfort of the glistening gold rings and bracelets, diamond necklaces, and chains, and crucifixes, and little charms. He takes in the cool beauty of rows of silver plated ornaments, and more silver filigree spoons and chains behind glass.

Here people choose and buy for their loved ones. Hagop can only be a voyeur of happy moments of indecision. This one. No. That one. She might like – Try it on. Yes, I think this one. Or, maybe – Because everything depends on what they choose. A wedding depends on the right ring, reconciliation depends on the right necklace, a good impression depends on the right present. This one – gift-wrapped. No, that one. Or perhaps this one – And Hagop the Armenian will look from one face to the other, or one finger to the other and give his expert advice. The women usually smile – the men not so often. Lost, some of them, in the choice process so loathed by males and so enjoyed by females. This one. No, I think that one … But never had any complaints, never, Hagop boasts.

Today his friend has come at the right time. It is a long hot afternoon and Onasagorou street is practically empty. So empty you can hear women's heels tick-tock, tick-tock. 'Poor old Haroutune,' thinks Hagop, wiping beads of sweat off his forehead. 'He looks awful, his hair all white, his shoulders forever hunched as if he's lost something on the floor. Poor old Haroutune, so tall and proud in his youth, reduced to a shuffler before his time.'

'So tell me, is there any movement? he asks, shaking the thoughts from his mind. Can you see any movement from up there, where you live?'

'Movement?'

'Yes, on the other side. They say things will happen.'

'What things?'

'I don't know. That they will finally come to an agreement …'

'I don't …'

'… now that we are nearly in Europe, you know, Europe, Haroutune! Did you ever think we Anatolians would ever become Europeans? Did you honestly ever think – But there are games …'

'Well …'

'… and tricks, and God knows what politicians are up to. And prices are shooting up … Drink, drink your coffee – and tell me, what have you been doing all this time? I haven't seen you – let me think –'

'I haven't …'

'It was at Christmas, wasn't it? At church? He pauses for a breath of a second and flashes a gold tooth in yet another smile. Ahhhh, Haroutune, we are getting old, my friend. Christmas, Easter, Christmas, Easter – and the years go by – and they never come back …'

'I …'

'But look on the bright side Haroutune, look at you. You're healthy, health is the most important, the most important thing. Everything else is secondary: money, wealth, property, all that is nothing – But you must come and see us some time and have some of my wife's baklava. She makes such wonderful baklava! What are you doing I tell her, are you trying to kill me? You know, it is possible to kill a man, I suppose, by overfeeding him, and she makes such wonderful finger-licking mouth-watering baklava –'

Haroutune looks at his watch.

'So when they told me there is this girl, her name is Makoush and she makes the most delicious baklava, of course, I set out on the way to her father's shop just 100 yards from here with my sweet tooth smile and I said to him I'm Hagop the jeweller and I want to marry your daughter and he said –'

Haroutune stops listening. The eternal optimist. Round-faced, red-cheeked, pot-bellied Hagop, without an ounce of malice or cruelty in him. There are times he harks back to that Haroutune would rather forget. The good times, the carefree times, the baklava times. The syrup of youth and love and such naïve proposals. I want to marry your daughter and her baklava. I am So and So's son and your daughter looks at me with such beautiful eyes. I want to take a photo of her long eyelashes and marry her forever and ever.

'Look, says Hagop, look. He unbuttons his shirt. Do you see? The scar? Open heart surgery.'

Haroutune has heard this story before. Many, many times.

'I nearly died, Haroutune. I went to hell and back. I lay on that hospital bed thinking of my wife and two girls and I nearly died. I prayed, and God heard me. After I came back from the dead, I swore I would go to church every Sunday and light a candle. And I've done it, Haroutune, every single

97

Sunday. And I thank God every single day for my wife with her heart of gold and my two daughters, my two diamonds …'

'How are they?'

'Fine, fine. One heavily pregnant, the other engaged … Such beauties, just like their mother! And next month, Insh-Allah, God willing, my first grandchild …'

'I've had a phone call …'

'I hope a son, Haroutune, the one I never – Phone call? Who from?'

'From Kevork.'

'Kevork Menoyian, the lawyer? What did he want?'

'No, no. My son Kevork.'

'Ah.'

Hagop is quiet. It is an effort for him to be quiet for more than a minute. But the subject of his friend's son is sensitive, so he keeps completely silent. Doesn't even ask: What did he say? What did he want? but his eyes search the lines on his friend's face for all the answers.

There is a sigh. Then:

'And before that there was a letter.'

'Ah.'

'He's getting divorced, Hagop – after fifteen years – he rings me to tell me he is getting divorced. We are incompatible, he says – took him fifteen years to realize they are incompatible. Six years, my only son, my own flesh and blood, Hagop, to write, to call, six years, can you believe it? I am ashamed to say it – ashamed –'

'Haroutune –'

'What do you think took Siranoush to the grave? Heartache, Hagop, heartache. Day and night she waited, she waited for a phone call, a letter from the other end of the earth, and he never wrote, he never called. His own mother, do you hear me, he killed –'

'No, no, Haroutune, stop –'

'And now I dream of her every night. And she asks me: Where is Kevork? Where is my Kevork? And I wake up, and I feel my heart will break into two. I lost my son a long time ago, Hagop. To some I say he is dead, he doesn't exist any more. And in my mind, it is true. But in my heart …'

'My friend, my friend, stop …'

'If it wasn't for Siranoush's memory, I would have put the phone down. I'd already ripped the letter into pieces, and now I'm thinking what to do, what to do –'

'Haroutune …'

'Because he is talking of coming back in the summer. To sort things out, he says. Sort things out! What a joke, what a bloody joke.'

A long time ago, Haroutune remembers, he was happy. What is happiness, he thinks today, an absent-minded look on his face. Some strange term invented by someone too stupid, or too young. Oh, but he was such a beautiful boy. He would grow up to be a pillar of strength. He would complete his studies abroad, and marry, and have children. He would make us proud. Yes, that's what we thought, that's what we wished for …

He takes out the photo album once again from its usual place, puts it on the coffee table and turns the pages one by one. Here he is, my boy. What a handsome boy he was! A good student, always respectful to his teachers, to us. How did this happen? Where did we go wrong? The more he searches for the answer, the angrier he gets. He can barely breathe, and clutches at his breast. He can feel his heart in his throat.

One day, soon, he thinks, he will open the door, and Kevork will be there, his head hanging down, the prodigal son. 'I have come back,' he will say. 'Father, forgive me.'

And he will tell his father the story of his squandered life.

'Father, I am sorry. I lived my life at your expense. I dropped out of university long before I told you. I just couldn't go on. I asked you for money, and gambled it away. I asked you for money, and used it on drugs. I lied to you. I am so sorry. Everything went wrong. Everything.'

He will look into his son's eyes, he thinks, and that will be the moment.

It will be the moment when all the photos he has ever taken will flash past his eyes. A whole lifetime, a series of black and white photographs, in the middle of a whirlwind. He will stand facing his son, and the photos will turn faster and faster, he will have nothing on which to support himself, and his life will suddenly start getting smaller and smaller. 'What have you done?' he will ask, in the faintest of voices. 'What have you done?', 'What have you done?', until he is so far away that he can no longer be heard.

My Silent Life

Baby started crying. She's always crying, as if she knows. As if she knows my silence must be broken.

'Baby's crying!' yelled my husband. I got up and walked away, past him, past the talking television, the tablecloth, the painting I won years ago. The lady across the road was watering her plants. 'How are you?' she said. 'I'm fine, I'm fine,' I said, shutting the door behind me. I walked away, non-stop. It felt as if somebody was timing me, timing my silently ticking life.

In my mind I was drafting poetry, beautiful verse about different things, but mainly sadness; Locked-In Syndrome, that sort of thing. 'Keep going, keep going!' That was my sports teacher at school, a long time ago, every Thursday. I remember his eyes and his cigarette-stained teeth and his bullying. I fell and broke my ankle. 'What can I do for you?' asked the doctor. 'What can I do for you?' I replied, showing him my knickers. The pink, flowery ones. There were flowers in the vase on his desk. Every time. I was emotionally plaster cast for life.

'Were you artificially inseminated?' asked my friend Tania. It's the type of question she would ask. 'I must have been,' I lied. Mother didn't like those questions. 'Rude. Ignorant. Repent. Repent and read the bible.' I did read it, aloud, and wondered if religion ever listened. 'Does your mother have a heart?' asked Tania. Good question. 'She must have,' I answered.

'How about your heart?' said the doctor, looking deep into Father's arteries. 'Just a few new ones and you'll be young again,' he smiled benignly. 'Thank you, Doctor,' said my father, the ninety-year-old sixty-year-old. 'For everything.' And the doctor threw me a sideways glance but I pretended it was dark and I couldn't see.

I once read a book about a man who couldn't find his wife. Disappeared – where? I wonder. Under the bed, behind the fridge, into the furniture, melted in the microwave, disappeared into his mind? He could not see her any more. My husband can't see me any more. We used to see each other every day, at school. My mother asked me once if we were seeing each other. 'Yes, we are,' I said. 'I see,' she replied, looking as if she had just chewed a bitter almond. 'That young man's not good enough for you. You're too good for him.'

'Don't you see,' asked Tania, 'that the doctor's abusing you?'

'How are you?' he asked, cupping my breast in his palm. Cold palms, like his stethoscope.

And so it goes on, the story of my mostly silent life. Silent, as if I'm underwater, swimming among sharks. Silent, as if I'm suffocating under my duvet. Silent, as if I'm deaf and dumb. 'Are you dumb?' asked Tania. I nodded assent. 'I meant dumb as in stupid,' she retorted.

Every night, the duvet covers my head and I breathe in and out, in and out, trying to get my voice out. It doesn't always play hide and seek. Sometimes it wants to play hangman – to hang my husband, or the doctor. Or both. At other times we go on treasure hunts together – in pursuit of happy loudness, boisterous songs, rippling laughter.

Was it a silly idea to run away? I've escaped from my husband and my screaming baby and I'm walking. Where to? Will I end up at the convent? 'Come in. come in,' said the Bad Witch to Hansel and Gretel. They went in licking their lollipops and were not seen for a very long time.

I remember my dream of a visit to the convent. The nun was feeding the cats in the courtyard. Black witch feeding her black cats. It was the height of summer. The doctor and I approached, hand in hand, wearing our swimming costumes. 'Shame! Shame!' she cried, pointing at me with a stick. 'Get out of here, dressed like a shit. You smell like a shit.

Screwing the man with you?' The doctor smiled serenely, like a saint.

'I would like some information on the convent,' I said, purposefully. 'We have no information,' she spat. 'On anything.'

'Not even religion?' I asked. 'I'm thinking of becoming a nun.'

'Do not taint this holy silence with your voice,' she hissed. 'And I can see your tongue's forced itself into various mouths. Shhh! Shhhooo!'

I woke up, as always hating myself for being so passive, even in my dreams. I should have hit her with her stick. I should have forced myself in. I should have stuck my tongue out at her, told her her breath smelt of stale bread. I should have made her lick the floor, her cats, her boots.

As I walk, I notice the trees look so healthy – spring trees. In blossom, strutting their stuff on Nature's catwalk. If they could talk, what would they say? As a reporter, I would record their answers and play them to the sky when it turned grey. I would do a Tania: 'Miss Nature, a lot of people seem to be saying that your Spring designs are a little too revealing this year. What is your reaction to that?' And Miss Nature would smile sweetly and say nothing at all. At all. 'Thank you for your comments, Miss Nature.' 'Not at all, not at all.'

I am now heading to my parents' house. In the

kitchen, will my voice come out like an energetic mouse amid my mother's flour and sugar, biscuits and bay leaves? Will it feel warm and safe there, like an unborn inside its mother's womb?

I remember my baby.

'Has your husband left you?' she asks, opening the door.

'I've left him.' I scream a silent scream. She doesn't hear me, of course. But she gives me a silent 'told you so' slap in the face. It hurts.

'More salad, anyone?' Silences. Polite. Rude. Coughs and potatoes. Father's arteries, shiny and bright, pump, pump, pump. He was an old man when he had that done. Now he is new. 'Thank you, Doctor, for everything.' That was a year ago; and a little more. 'Will you be your own bridesmaid?' asked Tania. 'I think so,' I replied. I wore white, inside and out. There's a picture on the mantelpiece. Smiling; outside, not in. Crying; inside, not out. Confetti and tears. Visible invisible. Hide and Seek.

'Coffee, anyone?' Which one of us is anyone? Anyone, anytwo, anythree? Mother Bear, Father Bear, Baby Bear? 'Who's been sleeping in my bed?' I ask. I've not been home for a long time. 'No-one,' says my mother, stirring prodigal into the coffee. Strange, that I was once her baby. 'When you start walking,' I once told mine, 'I hope you never trample on anyone.' It was said silently, but she started crying. She's always crying, as if she knows.

'Have you told Baby Daddy's a doctor?' asked Tania.

'I might,' I said. 'When I find my voice,' I thought.

Coffee Cup

I never believed in the coffee cup. On a school trip in June, many years ago, the toothless grin of the old lady drew us to her. We drank the coffee, turned over our cups and laughed at her pink gums. She picked up my cup with her arthritic, wooden fingers and lowered her face into my future. The other girls gathered round.

'Look inside this coffee cup and see the sediment of your life's patterns, which will tell you things about your future,' the toothless voice droned. 'Oh, yes, many, many patterns on the inside walls of the cup, just like ripples. There is a fish, you see, with its tail, and a boat sailing. There is a man in the boat sailing to you. Hurry up and see him. Meet him, hurry up – or else it will be winter.'

I told her I had all summer, all my life – to which she replied silence.

My mother listened bright-red, as if she had just been slapped in the face. 'You should never have gone near her,' she said, boiling with indignation, for she thought she knew my future better than anyone. 'She's a witch, that's what. There's one in every village. The devil dressed as a woman, stirring your fate and eating into your youth.'

She talked about it for weeks. Non-stop. She cleaned the house and talked about it; cooked and lit candles in church and talked about it. Remembered the incident and searched my eyes for clues of secret pacts with the witch. When my coffee cup was forgotten, and her anger subsided, she reverted to her daily habit of filling reminiscences of her own wasted youth with words. I knew the sequence well: 'At your age, I was married. At your age, I had you. At your age, I ...' She would never complete the sentence. There was nothing to complete it with. For a moment she would look embarrassed, and continue dusting. 'At your age,' I often thought, 'I hope I will have lived.' I was eighteen.

Years later I proved the truth told by the coffee cup. Perhaps I did it to spite my mother. I went to the old port deliberately looking for a man. After two failed engagements, I was the eccentric who had never loved, except once, 'the doctor who left her for a bigger dowry'. The village talked. I would give them more to talk about. Until there was no more to talk about. Soon.

When the peach sun melted into the evening and the cicada persisted in telling the world its shrill stories of boredom; when the sweat beaded a necklace of drops round my neck and the water hissed on the shore and splashed, as if sequin-tailed sirens were plunging into the Mediterranean; when the road tarmac oozed with the heat of the day and the pores of my skin opened up to the evening breeze – I met Ramez. His large olive eyes smiled, and we met.

'Here,' he said. 'This is my secret place. My fishing boat.'

Our bodies met. We held each other, and the wood and nets and sheets absorbed our heat under the dark supervision of night. It was my night in shining armour. 'I have never slept with a stranger,' I told him. 'I have never slept on the sea.' He hushed my hair with strokes of his big, dark hands. And over us the moon shone like a brightly polished silver coin. I listened, my heart full of stars, to the sound of his breath and mine. Nestling my face in his neck I finally slept and dreamt. That it was morning and I was collecting his clothes off the beach as if picking crabs, some deadly, some dead, asking Ramez if the sand would bite my bare feet; singing a wistful mermaid tune: '*When will I see you again? Perhaps tomorrow, perhaps never?*'

When we woke up we ate watermelon. He cut it into two and then into slices. Sitting on a half-broken chair, half-dressed and half-awake, I sucked at the last drops, stacking the black pips to one side; and wondered, as I watched his eyes, if he was a Spaniard, an Italian or just a man from the sea. The man that my coffee-cup had promised me.

'I wish,' I said, 'I wish I was happy.'

'I thought I made you happy,' he whispered, and took my hand. 'Don't cry.'

At the sound of his voice the salt of my tears turned to sugar, and a small joy sprinkled the vast expanse of the sea. I felt as fragile as a jasmine flower. He kissed my tongue with his cigarette breath and looked into my mascara-stained eyes, smiling awkwardly, inwardly, as if he wanted to help me but didn't know how. I thought then that I had never seen him smoke a cigarette and wished I had met him long ago, ten, twenty years ago, five months ago in my garden of youth. We would have drunk coffee under the eucalyptus tree, kissing in full view of the village, waving at my mother. And suddenly I remembered what the cause of my sorrow was. I had never dared in my life. I had never made a splash.

The clinical words came back to me. 'Five, six months, maximum. I'm sorry.' Ironically, words from the mouth that had jilted me. 'I'm sorry.'

The heat descended on us that month. You felt its crudeness, like a dog's bated breathing on your earlobe, the sweat salivating and dribbling on your body. Watermelon with Ramez breezed air-condition cool into my memory during the day and I returned to the boat every night. My mother's hot blast of Greek frequently interrupted my thoughts of nocturnal bliss. She talked to me in much the same way she talked to my father. Who left her. For bottles of brandy and a heart attack.

'You must tell me,' she said, 'if you're not well. You're pale. Despite the sun.'

'I don't,' I replied, 'think so.'

'Working too hard,' she went on, without listening, a faint flush of pink indignation forming on her round bun cheeks. 'Evening classes are doing you no good. No good at all.'

In the heat of summer, her words stung like mosquito bites. And not just hers. There were others who talked, nudged each other, peered out of their windows when I passed. My feelings rolled into prickly hedgehog balls.

'I caught some red mullet today,' said Ramez one night, 'but they didn't pay me much. I'm illegal.'

'Remember,' Mother said the following day, while chopping the salad, 'remember you are a Greek Orthodox.' There was a touch of bitter Fetta in her voice.

Perhaps she had seen me with Ramez. Followed him to his house, introduced her bun cheeks to the immigration office. Moonwhite in the darkness, conspired to ruin the one happy sediment in my coffee cup. It hadn't taken long for village talk to reach her.

It didn't take long for Ramez to appear on the early evening news. Along with a group of about twenty young, bearded, bewildered men. Trying to make sense of the commentary, snatching at the words 'arrested', 'illegal', 'foreigners'. Waiting to return. Ramez staring at me through the screen, watermelon pips falling through his fingers, black tears.

'Look at them! There may be babies in their houses,' her voice spat vinegar into the clot of anger forming in my throat. 'Lots of babies, crying, gooing and women nearly pregnant, tugging at their hair and crying out. I've heard they treat their women like dirt.' The whole village applauded.

It was the first time my mother heard me scream. It was also the last. Coffee cups and plates crashed like cymbals, becoming one with the salad. 'Here's the mess I've made of my life. You're standing in the middle of my chopped salad of a life. Well – I have very little of it left … so eat, mother, eat.'

I found the boat, but the sea seemed so rough without Ramez. The stark sky so cold. Hurry up – or else it will be winter. Who had said that? My mother, the witch, the doctor, Ramez? All the patterns, the words of my past merged into one. *At your age I had you. I have never slept on the sea. Perhaps tomorrow, perhaps never...*

Beneath the pink sky of dawn, coffee-coloured ripples carried me along. When I looked back, no land was visible. And for the first time in my life I was happy.

Next Year

Next year, my mother said, we will move. We will move out of the heat, the dust, the feet, the looks, the heat, the dust, the people, the words, the names following us. No, it's enough, we will move, she said. Next year it will be spring, we will breathe, there will be a green lawn like a carpet, a long clothesline for our clean new clothes, and cool breeze rooms for each one of you, and friends, dozens of them, to fill the house, and ice cream and ice cream. No, no, this is enough, the heat, the dust, I can't think any more it's in my head the feet, the looks, the people, the words, the same, the same, the same. I'm fed up. We will move. Next year.

She clung to her belief that things would change the same way she clung to us. I listened to her every word and believed it and dreamed and wanted all the things she wanted: a washing machine, a hairdryer, a dishwasher, a microwave, all those things that make life so easy and beautiful. We would win the Lotto without even playing it and be rich and have a father. Next year.

Yes, mama, we will move because of the heat, the sun, the dust and the noise.

We went to the dry river that coiled itself round the eucalypts and their fallen pale leaves. We walked everywhere jumping, galloping on the dry eucalypt leaves then on the dry field grass like little horses making more dust with our feet, jumping into the sea like little fish being born and coming to life with our yellow, blue, red, green caps. Put on your caps my mother cried, the sun! the heat! Put on your caps. Caps with blue, red, yellow, green coloured segments, like strange shells on the sand, sometimes blowing away in the wind before we could catch them.

Please tell me I asked the sea – which slid off my body drop by drop – please tell me I asked the sea – which made us look so small – please tell me where we can be happy next year. And the sea always seemed to be saying shhhhhhhhhhhhh … shhhhhhhhhhhhh … Telling me to be quiet, because I wanted to know too much. You have eaten up our father, so tell me, where have you hidden him? Shhhhhhhhhhhhh … said the sea.

It was one day in summer, during those interminable heat and dust days that the sea first spoke.

Next year never came. My mother shrivelled up as if something inside were eating her up. Her beautiful skin looked cracked and she looked so fragile with her broken porcelain skin and huge, brown, haunted eyes and her black hair hanging all over her shoulders, and the dresses hanging so big on her. We didn't know that death had chosen her and death made everything ugly and wrong. She had gone all wrong, her voice too weak, her arms so thin.

Death came and took her. We found her with her face slumped down on the kitchen table and we shook and shook her but nothing came out. She was empty. We screamed but she didn't move; we ran out, she didn't come after us; we ran in the heat, the dust, the sun, trying to find someone, anyone, to bring her back.

The people from Welfare came and the woman talked to us with words which had no meaning, only sound and she looked at us with her glasses perched on top of her nose, and said words and words but I could only make out 'sadly' 'now' 'your mother' and she was dressed in blue, light blue blouse and dark blue skirt and blue sandals. Ever since that day I've associated the colour blue with death. Death is blue and brings blue news. Sadly. Now. Your mother. You shed tears and you remember and you forget, and you want to remember, and you want to forget your mother's voice which says the heat, the sun, put on your caps, and her hands on the table, empty, and her eyes vacant and her voice dead, and the woman in blue comes like a devil, or an angel and tells you it's over, she's dead, now your mother, too.

When both your parents die you are a little blue orphan. Sadly, now, and this new word. Sadly, now, we were orphans, orphans, light blue sea, dark blue sky, orphans and we were moving to the city to be a-dopt-ed, a-pod-ted, it was a word she taught us this strange word which we sometimes got right and sometimes didn't.

Shhhhhhhhhh said the sea . Don't say the word too loud. You will wake up both your parents.

They took us to the city. Nikos, age 8. Maria, age 7. Nikos and Maria, Maria and Nikos brother and sister, sister and brother, holding hands, holding each other so close, so firmly, with that AND, until somebody said there should be no 'ands' so we couldn't hold hands, we couldn't be together, there had to be a full stop in between us, Mrs Irini at school said all sentences end with full stops. Nikos. Maria. Maria, full stop. Nikos, full stop.

They took me to a beautiful house where they had a washing machine and microwave and a lawn, and everybody smiled, and the woman said I could call her mama if I wanted to. I didn't want to. The house was clean, the house was big and beautiful, you should never look back, but I did. At the house by the sea, the heat, the sun, and the dust. When I wept the tears rolled out, down, silently, and those that didn't stayed inside me, somewhere, I don't know where, and many years later they came out.

Nikos. Nikos my brother Nikos every night it was a nightmare, a dream, he was pulling me into the sea. My mother was dancing with the waves, my father was laughing with the crows, and the house by the sea was empty, empty, its windows open and waves all round splashing in, splashing in, until it was all wet.

Does the sea ever end, or is it forever and ever, does the sea ever dry up, or is it forever and ever. Never and ever are so close and next year never came. Our mother was dead forever and ever and ever, like the sea forever and ever alive and blue and deep. Tears are so lonely like leaves fallen off branches. Orphans send kisses to each other in the wind but the kisses never meet and hang in the air not knowing which way to go until the wind blows this way, then that way, and they are lost like dreams when you wake up. Your mother kisses you in your sleep and you wake up with tears hot in your eyes, your ears, because next year never came.

But you grew up, shhhhhhhhhhhh … You grew up, shhhhhhhhhhh … in the big city. And even now, sometimes, in your car the sea seeps in slowly into the silence in your head and the emptiness of your heart shhhhhhhhh … Throat parched, thirst in the big city, heat and traffic lights, the sea moves in, first a trickle, then waves, then currents.

The traffic lights turn red and you look at yourself in the mirrors of the tall building distorted like so many years pressed into a can, melted and beaten like metal, like next year, next year, next year which never came.

Sweet & Sour

Once, I looked up all the words for sadness in different dictionaries in the library. Tristesse, Traurigkeit, tristeza … I wondered what sadness was in Chinese and remembered a Chinese student on a moped who had stopped me in the street to ask: 'Flat, rent, here?' and I had told him to look for the signs which said FOR RENT. On his moped, in the streets of Nicosia, he had looked so sad, so lost, so alone. Perhaps there was a long word for sadness in Chinese and I would have to look for it in their beautiful poems, search for it beneath each word, as if looking under the petals of a beautiful flower for the perfume, the meaning of life. The Chinese had such beautiful sayings. *Even summers have winter weather.*

Some of my friends made fun of them because they thought (they suspected) that the Chinese students in Nicosia eat dogs. 'There was a funny smell coming out of their flat,' a friend of mine once said. 'We couldn't get past those stairs for days on end, there was such a stench.' 'Only the other day I heard yelping behind the door, a dog scratching at the door to escape, I imagine …' 'And one of our neighbours' chihuahuas disappeared. They looked and looked but …'

Once, I saw a Chinese girl with a mobile phone pressed to her ear, sitting on the steps outside the college where she was studying. In seconds, her voice changed from the high-pitched incomprehensible gabble and giggle, that high pitch which dips its head in water and then comes up again to breathe – it always reminded me of a duck – into silence. In seconds, her voice stopped, just stopped and in its place was nothing. What was the girl listening to? Perhaps her father had died of a heart attack – perhaps her brother – in an accident in the army – her mother, of cancer. Many, many miles away, something had happened. Something which had made the Chinese girl's face now so still, so quiet, her eyes melting, her throat in knots, a still portrait. Then, a group of young Cypriots on motorbikes went past, one after the other, and made such a racket that she walked away from the spot where she had sat still for so long, disappeared round the corner and out of sight. *Do not mourn the people of the past, they are gone …*

That same night, on the news, I saw a report about a young Chinese student who had jumped off the roof of her block of flats on Arsinoe street in Acropolis. Her body, they said, was almost unidentifiable. None of her flat mates could guess the reason behind her act. She was always polite and friendly, and an excellent student.

Suddenly, I hear an old song,
Weeping, I wish for my home.

My News

I f you want to hear my news –
I've met somebody met split up met split up
these are the words in my vocabulary and he says
he loves me and I think I love him and once or twice
we went out though we were actually in and you
know after a drink or two I don't know how many
we ended up in bed having sex and he says he
adores me though I think that adore is a strong word
and a bit old-fashioned.

Anyway he whistles like I've never heard
anyone whistle before so I tell him I find it really
sexy so he whistles some more a tune from his
country he says. He comes from a place called
Noland Everyland Nowhereland Everywhereland
Perfectland Imperfectland pick and choose he says.
Wow that's so cool the way he makes up stories
about where he comes from I've never known a
man to do that and we sleep in each other's arms
cuddly coo coo like two pigeons in each other's
wings coo coo cuddly wuddly and there is a smile
on his lips even in his sleep.

So in the silence the stillness and the dark I think how every man is different every time is different I look at the ceiling the floor the floor the ceiling left right the alarm clock which shows the hours and minutes in green spaceship numbers the tassles on the bedspread move and so on. Sometimes you know I try to decide what love is when I am asleep and my heart is awake when he's asleep and his heart is awake and we're lying together like one when the two hearts speak and whisper and laugh and nudge and go whoops tick tick tock tock I suppose that's what love is though I can't really be sure.

We travelled places together. We went to Limassol to Larnaca Ayia Napa and even Kyrenia and his bedtime reading is books on wild animals. Seriously he reads about lions and tigers and hyenas with particular interest in how the males vie for attention from females how the peacock shows his tail etc. There's so much violence and bullying in the animal kingdom too he said it's just that we never see it. And once he said he'd watched a documentary in Australia about how male camels get all frothy in the mouth and fight each other vying for a female's attention.

It's the strangest thing seeing men fight over a woman. It happens all the time. She's mine no she's mine I saw her first. No I did. Punch kick wham bam whoosh punch kabam and another kick for good measure and the blood and the bruises and in the middle of it YOU the object of their desire running from one to the other shouting Stop Stop. One looks at you with blood trickling down his nose the other with a bruise under his eye and that madness which comes out in men's eyes when they are mad or angry. What happened to you someone will ask when they get home. Nothing. What happened to you when the other one gets home. Nothing. The answer is always nothing but you know you are the reason and feel kind of proud you have caused so much damage and they won't even be best friends any more because of you are you ashamed or guilty because it's all because of you. Perhaps you smiled too much at one or kissed the other too hard but how did all this happen it is all a mess it's a bloody mess and how did you get into it.

So the flesh has its comforts and discomforts and when you're sleeping tick tock tick tock none of this is apparent or visible. Everything is fine and safe and everything is a smile on your lips as you sleep. When you wake up you are still in love your hair all tousled and his face all bristles and one leg out and another one in one arm out and another one in and heaps of blankets on the floor and two pillows squashed together by one hand so there isn't enough pillow for the other one's head. Slowly you look at the time slowly and quietly you get up so you won't wake him up you realize he's awake under the pillow. What time is it. First question. What time is it. Under the pillow and one hand sticking out and the crumpled sheet longer at one end and shorter at the other. Quarter to eight. 7:45. That fully awake bitch Morning spreads herself out on the balcony peers in and wonders if you're still in bed. You can't hear your heart any more only the whooooshhh of the shower and the zzzzzzzz of the electric shaver and the clock tick tock tick tock knock knock knock of morning.

You wake up in the morning. You have to wake up in the morning. Because if you didn't I suppose you would be comatose or even dead. But you are alive so you get up and look at the morning through the window. There in front of you is the long day.

The news is that last night was magic and we were getting married. But this morning I'm not so sure.

Mr Boom Boom

I ask my friend Mar to tell me the true meaning of love. She's a little older than me and has a great deal more experience with (shhh!), you know, MEN.

Mar is short for Maria. She prefers it she says because in Spanish, you know, Mar means the sea, it makes her feel exotic.

Mar, I say, tell me about love. When you love someone are you sure they love you back?

Well, she says, self-importantly, because she loves putting on the teacher act with me. Well, the point is, you never really know for sure, but 90% of the time you can tell.

And the rest of the time?

The rest of the time is a waste of time because, you know, nothing's happening, nothing's moving, the phone's not ringing, you don't see stars and you can't hear the boom boom.

Boom boom?

Yeah, of his heart. You have to listen carefully for the signs of the boom boom. Usually his face takes on a different colour like red or pink or somewhere in between – a kind of hot colour anyway …

Oh, okay. (We've learnt hot and cold colours at school.) Like a kind of red and blue together, right?

Yeah, yeah, right. Kind of – You don't really see it in the dark but you feel it, and when you hear the boom boom, then you know –

What?

Well, his – you know – dick – is going hard.

Hard?

Yeah, like a kind of banana or cucumber or something.

Really?

Yeah, going dead hard.

Can you touch it?

Well, yeah. You can, but you have to do it carefully and gently because it's like a little animal, you know, at first. And THEN it becomes a beast.

Oh Mar! Knock it off! Tell me the truth.

It's true. I swear. It just goes hard and becomes a beast and that's when he wants to come into your clothes and rip you apart and eat you. That's when your knickers come off and your clothes start falling off, off and then it comes in, in, in to get you.

And then?

Well, it's hard to explain. Things happen, you know, you start rubbing and making noises.

Noises? What kind of noises?

Like angry or painful or something. I don't know, noises.

Oh my GOD. Like in films?

Exactly like in films.

Then what?

Then, well, you make noises then they get louder and louder as if the whole room is filled with them.

And then?

Then, sighs Mar. That's it.

That's it?

Yeah, you say bye bye to your boom boom lover and you go home.

What? That's the meaning of true love? Isn't that just – you know – (shhh!) SEX?

What's the difference, laughs Mar. Love, sex, sex, love, they just invented two words for the same thing.

But when do you know if it's the right – you know – time or if he's – you know – right for you.

Stop talking like my mother, will you? says Mar blowing smoke all over my face. Look. There is no Mr Right or Mr Wrong. There is just Mr Boom Boom. You hear Boom Boom, you get laid. That's it.

So we finish our burgers and fries. Mar licks her fingers (there is not a single one which doesn't have a ring on). I wipe my mouth with a serviette. Mar gives me a funny look and we leave.

I've got to get a few things at the pharmacy, she says, and laughs. I have no idea what she means. Oh okay, I'll just catch the bus. I'm already late.

And as she walks away on her high heels I swear I notice a man in a business suit adjust his tie and turn to give her a kind of – you know – look.

Bus number 12 comes and I get on. Good, plenty of empty seats so I can sit by the window and look out at the world. Oh! Look at the time – quarter to five already – they'll be waiting – I'll just say there was an accident on the way and all the roads were blocked.

Somebody is sitting next to me. A guy in jeans with his legs wide apart and size 44 trainers. He's about my age and is holding a computer magazine. I give him a surreptitious look when he's not looking. He'd be quite good-looking if it wasn't for the zits which cover most of his face. I try to make out the colour. Red? Pink? Purple? Oh my GOD! Definitely purple and – I mustn't look at – you know – so I just listen to the boom boom (yes!) the boom boom of his heart. Oh my GOD! Could it be the little animal becoming a beast? Wait till Mar hears this! At the next stop he gets off, but I'm sure we'll meet again. I always take this bus. I smile and almost wave and smile again from where I'm sitting, but he pretends he doesn't see me, and crosses the road. His big feet and his heart go boom boom across the road.

Now my thoughts turn to THEM – you know – my parents. My father with his money worries and my mother with her health worries – worries, worries, worries, worries that's what our house is filled with – even our furniture has that worried look. When I open the door, the questions start where have you been do you know what time it is what do you think you're doing are you trying to kill us have you no consideration at all why didn't you ring us didn't it cross your mind we were worried sick worried worried worried. I answer calmly (I surprise myself sometimes at how calmly and clearly I can articulate lies): I went to the library to work on a school project and before I knew it it was dark and I couldn't find a call box then on my way here there was an accident and traffic and diversions and –

I go into my room and close the door. I smile and take my mobile phone out of its secret place and text Mar:

Thx Mar! Met Mr Boom Boom 2day.

The Day before Yesterday

The day before yesterday was different from today.

Somewhere a long time ago yesterday or the day before she killed herself my friend the manic depressive the day looks so different today please help me please help me she said I was going through my menopause and he slept with a younger woman I love and hate I loved him I hated him and sometimes both and sometimes neither. I listened and couldn't think of anything useful to say don't kill yourself men are not worth it we love them and hate them don't do it I know it is hard to pretend you are not hurt men are such bastards but you are a poet you have a voice don't kill yourself he is not worth it. She listened with her eyes getting cooler and cooler I think she hated me for trying to put her off today the weather is chillier and she is dead and under the earth I wish I could change things and she is dead she could not change her life just end it she killed herself with gas or with a noose the day before yesterday they said she was a good person but they didn't say she was a good woman she was mad and mad and sad and bad all the rhyming words she couldn't take care of her own children she abandoned them poor man what could he possibly do he married a mad woman he couldn't keep her in the attic lock her up locked up all the time. She's abandoned them now for good they didn't couldn't see how hard she tried how bitterly she cried how often she thought her life must end must start all over again but differently. She would meet the right man and have the right children and live happily happily ever after. They said it was possible the psychiatrist said it is possible to make the impossible happen. Oh my God oh my God oh my God she has killed herself she killed herself sometime between the day before yesterday and today the autopsy showed it was the day before yesterday and she will never see the day after tomorrow.

The day before yesterday I had no children but today I am in bed with a baby a pink baby which smiles and coughs and sometimes shows its tiny tongue. My son will change my life I just know it he will change the world. I will be a single parent we will go places together to the supermarket and he'll sit on the trolley we'll go to the zoo and he'll point at gorillas we will go to the airport and he will watch planes take off and one day I'll tell him I love him I really love him when I sit in a waiting room and wait for him to be treated for his addiction I will wait and wait for nine months for him to arrive and then one day he will tell me he didn't really want to live and why did I have him why was I so cruel he didn't believe in life in God in anything and why was I speaking to him when he wanted to be alone alone alone leave me alone just leave me alone he cried alone with his syringes the room with no light leave me alone ma. Here he is my baby my pink little baby with his tiny little red tongue which showed when he yawned after sucking my milk with his tiny little lips. The day before yesterday he wasn't even here didn't even exist and today he isn't even here doesn't even exist.

My neighbour had a dog he slept with her they were a couple she went everywhere with him. She was twelve years old and diagnosed with cancer. He went to pharmacies tried to prolong her life with forbidden drugs pretended they were for him to try and prolong his own life he pretended everything would be fine but she had a tumour in her head he loved her more than any human he loved her more than anyone loved her the way he had loved no woman. She spoke to him when he went away she refused to eat when he walked away she whimpered she had chocolate brown eyes the saddest you have ever seen and the black coat of a little black lamb. Yes he told me today about the dog out of the blue about this dog I never met the dog is more important than anything he told me and I am preparing for a funeral the day after tomorrow. When I kiss a woman he says I remember her when I taste a woman yes my bitch my wonderful little bitch returns to lick my face lick my neck so I feel alive she sniffs my skin. Take your clothes off he tells me out of the blue so I can admire your youth your body. I have seen you walking up and down these stairs I am not alone I have a wife but we live separate lives she was once young like you came into my life knocked on the door and wanted philosophy lessons I can teach you nothing about anything I told her I am an old man I was old even then I was young please go away I said to the young woman who became my wife please stay. Two days ago I could still hear my heart beating and loved the way the wind leant on my face when I was out for walks with my dog in places she discovered and I followed but you are young do you understand how an old man can be in love with his dog have you ever wiped the rain off a dog's coat have you ever smiled at whimpers have you ever been in love with a bark but let us not get too attached. I don't want to tell you this but I am lost without my dog when she died I stopped eating I stopped feeling for days months please go away. The day before yesterday I could still hear my heart beating and today I am not even sure if I am alive.

The Garden Restaurant

I am as tall as the tables in the restaurant, perhaps a little taller, because I can rest my elbows on the tables, and pretend to be playing - when, in fact, I am looking at my mother and that smile on her face. She's smiling at the man I have come to know as my uncle.

Uncle Takis makes me laugh, but he makes mum laugh even more. I put on my nice dress and we visit him. When we come home at night and we are alone, mum wears her injured look as she takes off her clothes.

She sits in front of the television blowing smoke rings in front of her eyes, and they are usually half closed, but she opens them when she realizes I am standing in front of her, looking at her. Then she puts out her cigarette, switches off the TV, takes me to my room, tucks me in, kisses me goodnight and switches off the lights. Before I go to sleep I pray that she will never die like my daddy.

Sometimes, Uncle Takis comes to visit us, too, and he and mum talk and talk. 'Taki mou,' she says to him, and I don't understand that, since he is not hers, how can he be her Taki? 'Taki mou,' she says, and sometimes sighs and looks at me.

So. Here we are one cold lemonade day, and mum is talking to Uncle Takis and somebody's dog is lying in the shade and mum says not to touch it, or else to go and wash my hands, and she gets impatient, because she has to look at me when I'm with the dog, and I think she'd rather be looking at Uncle Takis.

'Whose brother is he?' asked my friends at school, at first, when Uncle Takis came to pick me up. 'Whose brother? Your mother's or father's?' So I made up a story: that he is dad's brother and that my dad is sick in hospital, and mum goes to visit him every day and Uncle Takis picks me up and takes me home and helps me with my homework and will even buy me a dog to protect me and my mum when we are alone at night. Until dad comes home.

The truth is, my dad died even before I was born – mum says.

The waiter approaches our table and we are all happy. I think especially mum. Her name is Eftichia, it means happiness. She is suntanned and beautiful and she's wearing that pink and white dress with the straps which sometimes come off her shoulder. She orders a beer and lights a cigarette.

Then Uncle Takis lights one too, and even though there is a small ashtray, they flick their ashes on the ground, and it doesn't really matter because we are outside in the garden of 'The Garden Restaurant'.

'What shall we eat?' asks mum. When she says 'we' she means me. Usually we have a toasted sandwich and chips and watch all the tourists here on Saturday because I don't have school and it's a treat, but today I don't know, so I shrug my shoulders. The ketchup has made rings on the tablecloth like mum's earrings.

I whisper something in her ear. Her face changes and she says 'Will you stop being silly? Just stop it, will you?' because what I've whispered is that I've just seen my daddy, down by the lake, near the ducks. Look daddy, it's me. Look daddy, I'm here, I whisper. Turn round so they can see you, daddy. Please.

Flight to Tel-Aviv

I love you love you so much Ahuvi I am on my way to you you will see me soon. What will I say how are you fine fine *ma shlomkha tov tov* all those words I have learnt like a good student I will ask my way to Tel-Aviv centre can you tell me the way to Dizengoff Street tell-a-viv tela-viv. I look different have become another person but I know you will recognize me I am blonde now used to be dark when you open the door what will you think.

Oh I hope. I hope you will Tell-Me I love you *ani ohev otakh* and I will Tell-You *ani ohevet otkha* and Tel-Aviv will be the most beautiful place in the world the biggest craziest widest wildest city where I will meet you once more Ahuvi. I am travelling to you can you believe it after so many months maybe years maybe centuries. I repeat all these words all these words so I won't forget so I can tell you I love you in Hebrew Ahuvi ani ohevet otkha after so long we will meet again.

I have you in my bag. I want to tell the man sitting next to me to wipe that depressed 9th of Av look that *partzuf shel tishea beav* off his face and to smile. Want to tell him that I keep my love in my bag here is my Ahuvi when he was in the volleyball team a long time ago do you see back row second from the left he has a small smile do you see he only smiles small smiles but he will smile widely when he sees me oh yes wait and see.

During the one hour flight I think of a hundred things we will do I am thinking let's swim let's float in the Dead Sea let's make it come alive let's read Amichai in the desert let's go to a Bar Mitzvah party let's sit and eat chicken soup and cholent and drink Carmel Mizrakhi wine and get drunk let's go to a kibbutz let's feed some stray cats paint a few walls climb the Golan Heights and dance to Ehud Banai –

Oh and what if. And what if none of this ever happens what if we don't. The man next to me is coughing can he read my mind does he know where I'm going does he know why I'm smiling can he guess why I'm writing all this has he read the novel of my life does he know the ending of this beautiful tale. I will ask him. He has stopped coughing and I have stopped at what if. Excuse me can you tell me excuse me do you know the answer to what if –

He is not even looking at me doesn't even know I exist Ahuvi he is not interested in anyone's life except his own keeps looking out of his own window at the white clouds and sighing white sighs. Wipe that 9th of August look off your face and try to smile just once during this flight there are just a few minutes left they have just announced Please fasten your seat belts   *na lehadek et khagorot hamoshav shelakhem* try to look as if today is the day you have been waiting for all your life today is the day that has taken off and is about to land today things will happen   Please fasten your seat belts *Eser Tesha Shmone* Ten Nine Eight Oh Ahuvi *Sheva Shesh Khamesh* Seven Six Five why am I counting backwards why am I counting we are not taking off we are landing Welcome to Tel-Aviv *Brukhim habaim le Tel-Aviv* –

Today is the beginning of the rest of your life.

My Armenian Nose

He tells me I have a beautiful nose. Especially in profile, he says, it shows strength of character. Not a teeny-weeny Anglo-Saxon nose, but an Armenian one in its full glory. Sometimes we stand in front of the mirror and compare the size of our noses. David is Jewish, so he has a Jewish nose – no smaller than mine, just slightly more hooked.

The fact that I am writing about it means I am worried. More worried than when I was twelve and realized at Marie McCarthy's birthday party that I had the biggest nose in the whole class … More worried than when I started looking at people's noses instead of their eyes while talking to them … And even more worried than when my first boyfriend cracked a big-nose joke and later said he didn't mean it.

(Well, whadyaknow? says an American actor on the screen. Well, well, well … he says slowly, as if he now knows all the answers to the biggest mysteries in the universe. Well, well, whatdyaknow. What does he know, exactly?)

But to return to the original problem: I am

worried about our children (if we get married, if we have any) who will they take after? They don't stand a chance, not the tiniest little nose chance in hell. Big noses will be in their genes. And who will smile at a pretty little girl with a big nose, and who in her right mind will fall for a big-nosed megalomaniac?

(I hate all those words which end in -iac. Megalomaniac, Hypochondriac, -iac, -iac, yuck.)

It is true, I am obsessed with my nose. Once I told David: 'I'm thinking of plastic surgery, everyone's doing it, shouldn't cost too much. I have already looked in my mum's women's magazines. On the back pages.' All David can say to that is to bend over my face and kiss my nose. 'I think it is beautiful,' he says. 'You should never get rid of beautiful things.'

So we're stuck with an Armenian-Jewish nose or a Jewish-Armenian nose. Jews and Armenians, we have histories and we have noses, we have tragedies and we have noses. We have beautiful and ugly. 'Look at Barbra Streisand,' says David's mum. 'Look at Charles Aznavour,' says mine. 'Yes,' I reply, 'but don't you see that they have beautiful voices to make up for their noses, or at least to detract people's attention from them?'

(Once I was travelling on the London Underground, and was woken up from my daydream – or nightdream, because it was night – when a sweet old man wearing a beret suddenly said: What's a nice Jewish girl like you travelling alone in London so late at night? I didn't have the heart to tell him I wasn't really Jewish, it was just my nose, and it wasn't really that late and could he mind his own business, so I just smiled and said: Got carried away shopping. To which he replied: Next time don't spend all your money in the shops – good Jewish advice.)

Let me tell you how we met. I mean David and I. We met in the lift, on our way to the fourth floor, inhaling the foul smell of cigarette smoke left behind by a man who got off on the second floor. 'I think it's awful,' he said, and I wondered what he meant, because he was looking straight at me. 'Yes, I know,' I said, still not knowing whether he meant my face, or the lift, or his life in general. 'I don't smoke. My name is David.' That's how he introduced himself, and I just had to say 'Well, I'm glad to hear it.' And that's how it all started, that's how we got to know each other. Whenever I think back to that night, I just have to smile, because you really must agree that it was wonderful, such a great way to meet.

Months later, I introduced him (no, the idea of him) to my family. 'A Jew?' my father shouted, while everyone else in the family started leaving the room. 'A bloody Jew? Oh, I see … Armenians not good enough for you now!' And he banged his fist on the table and all the glasses shook. 'An Armenian?' cried Mrs Cohen (my future mother-in-law, fingers crossed) as if she had just seen a ghost, and her hands shook. 'An Ar-me-ni-an? What the hell are you trying to say to me, David? Jewish girls not good enough for you now?' David told me this while we lay awake together in bed and gently breathed in the night air, and we agreed there and then that one day we would produce a beautiful creature together. A beautiful Armenian Jew or Jewish Armenian with the cutest little face and the brightest brain in the world.

One beautiful summer day, when the sun is shining, the sea is blue and the sky is clear … I will tell the beautiful creature about the night I met his/her father, I will tell him/her about the lift and the cigarettes and the smoke, about my dreams of Bar/Bat Mitzvahs and pomegranates, symbols and books and various alphabets that I plan to teach him/her. About how the glasses shook when my father found out, about the way Mrs Cohen's hands shook when she found out, about how worried I am about him/her because after all I am a Jewish/Armenian mother and that's part of their job, the reason for their existence is to worry about their children. And he/she will look at me as if I am SUCH a silly child, and he/she is SUCH a clever adult. He/she will shake his/her head knowingly, and say in an American accent (I have no idea why I like American accents): 'Well, well, well… whatdyaknow, Ma. Whatdyaknow.' As if to say, can I possibly be the offspring of this silly woman? And I will read his/her mind and reply with a smile: 'Oh yes, baby, just look at the size of your nose.'

And I just hope he or she will smile back.

Okay, Daisy, Finish

Daisy hums a tune to herself as she cleans the studio. There is not so much to do here. Mr Andreas has told her not to touch the paintings, but to wash all the plates and glasses, remove the old newspapers, sweep the floor. She also cleans the small toilet at the back and the dusty balcony at the front. At this time of the afternoon, the sun glares at the clutter of tubes of paints, and she fears they will melt all over the table. But he has told her not to touch them. She also daren't touch any of the hundreds of brushes of different sizes, sticking out like little puppets out of old Nescafé tins, as if touching them might bring them to life.

He is so untidy, this Mr Andreas, says Daisy, rather affectionately, as if she is talking about a naughty child, and bends under the table to pick up some magazines and an ashtray brimming with cigarette stubs. Two thin magazines have been placed under one foot of the table to stop it from wobbling and another flops over a lamp, and a woman's hat hangs from the edge of the tap of the tiny sink. Inside the sink she makes out a trail of black ants climbing a small mountain of spilt white sugar and dregs of coffee.

Daisy looks forward to the sound of the key in the door, at this time every week. A clink, a click, a turn, and they are in front of her. Such a scruffy man, always wearing an old shirt and jeans when he's painting. Must have been good-looking in his time. Even now that his hair and beard are greying, his eyes are a very deep blue and so unusual for a Cypriot. And women stick to him as if he's made of honey …

Daisy pretends to be working, but knows he will soon want her out the way – and will soon dismiss her with Okay, Daisy, finish. The three words of her salvation. Okay. Daisy. Finish. Which basically mean: Go for a walk for a couple of hours, because I now need this studio. You can finish cleaning it later.

She doesn't know whether to smile, or to pretend she hasn't heard, to annoy him slightly, so he'll have to repeat the same words. Okay, Daisy, finish.

Okay, Daisy, finish, says Mr Andreas, taking the woman's coat. There is the slightest touch of emphasis in the 'i' of 'fin', which makes her quietly abandon broom and duster, nod acquiescently, and make towards the door. But not before she's had a look at her.

They must have been drinking at lunchtime, her look is vague, distant, but she is not his usual type.

Not as tall, not totally blond. (Such cold eyes, thinks Daisy, like ice). But certainly Russian, like all the others. They will go into the studio now, and he will undress her and paint her, or paint her and undress her. He with his hairy arms, the Cypriot, and she the smooth Russian.

And Madam is having her nails done, because today is Saturday, and they are going out tonight.

Okay, Daisy, finish. Daisy goes out for a walk. Takes herself for a walk, and is grateful. For the extra time, the free time, the walking time, the thinking time. Step after step, she thinks of her fiancé in Sri Lanka. She thinks, walks, walks, thinks. Of another city, of another time, of other people. Of another Daisy. *Things I will bring you ...* A Greek song blares out of a parked car with a running engine, and nobody in it ... *Jewels and gold and dreams from another land* ... She doesn't understand the words, but the wistful melody keeps pace with her footsteps, and her own language, asleep in her throat chokes as it speaks to her mind. Home. My home. That feeling again in the pit of her stomach. The sickness exactly as it is described in dictionaries.

Homesickness, n., homesick, adj.

The colours, she thinks. They are different here. The sounds. The wind. If I could remember the exact green of the leaves, the exact taste of the mango, if I could feel the monsoon on my face again. If I could go to the market and lean against each stall and take in each of the smells and take shelter when the brooding skies break open, and then run … If I could be kissed again and take off the sari clinging to my body and my bangles and – What time is it? She looks at her watch. Okay, Daisy, finish.

Soon she must return to a studio full of cigarette smoke, the smell of paint and turpentine, an old table where colours have been mixed and tested, a half finished painting of a naked woman, parts of her just painted, a couch where love has recently been made.

Daisy mops the marble floor absent-mindedly. Her mind is elsewhere and she doesn't care if there are stains she has missed, because it is not important. The important thing is to be seen working, seen, not heard, because you are only Daisy, only a maid to them, she says to herself. But I know things about this household, things that nobody else knows, nobody.

And she mops sloppily, sloppily, water dripping from the edge of each marble stair, until she feels the presence of somebody behind her, at her shoulder.

Madam, she says, I finish salon now.

Daisy, says Madam, how many times I've told you be careful? Do the mop slowly, less water?

Sorry, Madam, says Daisy. Less water, okay.

Madam says something in Greek into her mobile phone – it is a word of disgust, then a word or two of anger – and her face, as she utters the words, is not a pretty sight.

No Madam, thinks Daisy, you are not a pretty sight. That is why your husband never paints you.

Speak of the devil and he will appear. Mr Andreas walks in and says Agapi mou, ('Agapi mou' means 'my love', thinks Daisy, and smiles at her mop) sorry I am late. But I had a meeting at the gallery about the exhibition, and –

You're always late! cries Maria Madam running her index finger over the top of the freshly polished dinner table and examining her fingertip for grains of dust. Always late! And there's the dinner party and I still haven't decided what to wear. And that bitch Lina has just called to say she can't come because something has come up and she's flying to London early tomorrow morning and – and – and – Daisy! Still mopping? Go to the kitchen and make sure everything is under control. There are important people coming tonight (you FOOL, she adds under her breath) and Andrea mou, make sure you sit next to Panos Xenofontos the contractor. They're building a beautiful hotel in Pafos and –

Andreas is already on his way upstairs. He regrets setting foot in any room where his wife is in full talking mode. She controls me, yes. I married her money, yes. I don't love her, no. But I think I may have liked her once, long ago. Long, long ago he thinks, and yawns, and steps into the shower.

Daisy wakes up. Daisy works. Daisy eats. Daisy sleeps. Daisy lives below ground in a beautiful basement, with her own shower, her own little stove, her own wardrobe, her own walls. Daisy writes letters home. Sometimes, she writes them in her mind while she takes the dogs for a walk at night. And the ones she writes in her mind are never posted.

My dearest Linton,
They treat me like dirt. But it doesn't matter. Because I will soon be back. With you. And we will get married and have as many children as you want.

Linton my love,
Today I thought of you while I was cooking for them, and I burst into tears. I heated the oil in the pan and started frying the chopped onions. Then, in my imagination, I added the cinnamon, the coriander, the cumin, and all those spices which are absent from my life, and as I tipped the chicken in, I thought of rice and dhal and patties and red chilli and my thoughts turned to you, and I started crying, but soon had to stop because she came in to ask how long dinner would be.

My lovely Linton,

I am saving all my money. That's why I haven't phoned you from the call box, or even bought a mobile phone, though all my friends have one. I prefer to write, go to the post office, stick the stamps on the envelope, knowing that you will be happy to find it in your letterbox, and wonder what is in it.

I make money here, Linton – but, you know? My life is not worth a rupee without you.

Love, Daisy.

She writes the letters, and seals them in her memory. One day, she hopes, her life will be okay, she will be beautiful Daisy, and all her troubles will finish. Okay, Daisy, finish.

She switches off the light and, as on many nights, in the dark, her eyes open, dreams of that day.

The clink, the click, the turn – but he is on his own. And the three words of her salvation – okay, Daisy, finish – remain unsaid. Unusual, thinks Daisy, and is slightly annoyed, because she has come to look forward to her walk at this time every week. Unusual, and there is something strange – restless – about the way he is moving around the small studio, from one painting to another, without saying anything to her, almost as if he is looking for something he cannot find.

But she says nothing. She has no right to ask or speak. You are only Daisy, only the maid, she says to herself. And if he doesn't want you to Okay, Daisy, Finish today, then you won't. She continues pretending to dust, then takes some wine glasses and dirty dishes off the table, and carries them to the small sink to wash.

First, he gets on his knees and bends over an enormous, half-finished canvas on the floor; he gets up shaking his head, then walks to one of the walls against which about fifteen or twenty of them are leaning upright, and starts looking at them with his head turned sideways.

Then he sits on the couch, puts his head in his hands and looks down at the floor. Something is wrong. Something is missing. A colour, perhaps – he is not sure. He has painted sameness, facelessness, pale bodies all merging into one. The eroticism, he thinks, is gone, when you've painted so many. The feeling is lost when you've screwed so many.

'He paints women in gentle colours, holding the mirror up to the fair sex,' some useless critic had once written about him. What absolute crap! What useless idiots they all were! Fools, flocking like sheep to his exhibitions. Marvellous, Andrea! Congratulations! Your best so far! You have exceeded all our expectations! And he cringed to think that he, the star student at St Martin's School of Art in the 1980s had ended up painting, two decades later, decorative bodies for people to hang up in their living room.

And this time round: thirty-five pieces of Russian flesh. Five women, seven sessions each. He lights a cigarette and remembers the last time he was here. He blows out smoke, half-closing his eyes. If only – some woman – harmless – just to pose – a different kind of woman – who asks for nothing in return –

He opens his eyes and turns to the sink.

Daisy, he says. Come here.

... Congratulations, once again, to Andreas Stephanides for his wonderfully refreshing new work. May he long continue to contribute to the arts scene in Cyprus, as well as abroad, with his remarkable talent and originality.

Applause.

The exhibition is now officially open.

The two men shake hands and pose for the press photographers. Andreas Stephanides, left. Andreas Orphanou, MP, right.

Applause.

In the stifling atmosphere of Zoë Gallery, on one of the first really warm evenings of the year, about two hundred people admire and applaud, shake hands with each other, kiss the air next to each other's cheeks, exchange the latest in gossip, smile beautifully at the cameras – we are the beautiful people, beyond any shadow of a doubt, yes, extremely beautiful – and perhaps even try to discern which of the ladies is still wearing her winter shoes. It is Spring, my dear, hadn't you noticed?

And the paintings hang all around on the walls. A few people – mostly men – are now going round with the titles and price list in their hand. Ah yes, Andrea mou, such beautiful paintings, such beautiful women! A few red stickers appear. What an imagination, what brushstrokes! More red stickers. They remind Andreas Stephanides of little clowns' noses, because this is a joke. This is all a farce, he thinks, and wishes he weren't sweating so profusely on this warm evening, as he listens, and nods, and circulates and shakes hands. Aphrodite is what you had in mind, I'm sure, Andrea mou – so meaningful, and what purity of colours! Exclamation mark after exclamation mark after exclamation mark stands and stares at naked women in pornographic poses – legs wide open, erect nipples on full breasts, facial features covered between wisps of hair – yes, wonderful, Andrea mou. And exhibit number 36? Ah. This is a little different. Dark Woman £1500. Mmmm. A little too dark for me.

Andreas wipes his forehead with his handkerchief. It is between the wiping and the replacing of the handkerchief in his pocket that he notices in the distance, holding a glass of red wine, standing next to the journalist Mimis Petrou, a vaguely familiar figure dressed in a pink sweater and black skirt with her back to him, a vaguely familiar hairstyle, and as she turns round to give him a very familiar look, he sees his wife approaching with a group of ladies from her Thursday morning coffee circle.

Andrea mou, says Maria Stephanides, my friends want a grand tour by the grand master. Would you? They're always telling me how lucky I am to be married to Picasso.

Andreas smiles obligingly at a group of women aged between 45 and 50, who are looking at him with the same faithful look he sometimes gets from his two dogs. Of course, he says, of course. This way, ladies. Shit. What the fuck is the Russian whore doing with Orphanou? – well, as you can see – What is he telling her, and what is she telling him? – the woman's beauty is a kind of still life in itself – and more to the point, did they come in together? – which, placed against the background of the mundane –

Somebody decides to buy Dark Woman and the gallery owner Mrs Zoe Ioannou looks for Andreas Stephanides. He is on the lower floor, somebody says, he's giving a guided tour. Two young men jostle among the crowd to reach the table with the drinks. Somebody almost spills red wine on a lady's white suit, and a portly gentleman of a certain age reaches his hand out for yet another canapé. And while Mrs Zoe is placing the red sticker next to the oil canvas depicting Daisy, Maria Stephanides approaches, and stops short, almost choking on the cucumber canapé.

It is the first time she is looking at the paintings. There was a time when she used to go through them with him, helping him select, reject, choose, give titles, set prices – but a long time ago, she thinks, such a long time ago, somewhere in the past, and now –

She stares in disbelief at a painting of a partially dressed woman whose skin colour, long jet-black hair covering her face, whose figure lying indecently on her stomach against a background of bougainvillea in full blossom – indicate that she can only be –

Maria mou, says one of her coffee circle friends. I just love this one. It's just so – kind of – primitive. A bit like Gauguin and those girls in Tahiti. You are married to a genius.

Are you out of your mind? cries Maria Stephanides, once they are inside the BMW. Are you out of your fucking mind? The maid, now? The filthy, fucking Sri Lankan? That filthy slut, you bastard?

Each word comes out as a shriek, and Maria Stephanides is sobbing, crying, shedding years of false words and promises and vows. Her shoulders shake, the tears transform her into a human being. The more she cries, the more the veneer is washed off her life and the paint of her former self runs down her cheeks while he keeps saying but I didn't, we didn't, it was just a painting, I didn't touch her. The more he says it, the more she cries, and ironically it is the only time in his life he is telling her the truth, and it is the only time in her life that she doesn't believe him.

The night is the night of the red and green traffic lights. He tries to concentrate and overtakes and is overtaken on the long Nicosia avenues, past the colourful shop signs, the crowded outdoor cafés ...

You bastard, she whispers now to her palms in front of her mouth, you fucking bastard, everyone, everyone knows, everyone, from now on – from now on – if it wasn't for the children – and that filthy whore leaves tomorrow, that dirty bitch and her filthy black skin leave tomorrow, do you hear me.

But she didn't he begins, driving like a blind man, and remembers the horror in the maid's eyes that Saturday afternoon, recalls how she had refused, how he had told her everything would be fine, how she had sat shaking for an hour, trying to cover her body with her long black hair, how eventually she had broken down into tears. And he hadn't even touched her, not even to console her, had just said Okay, Daisy, finish, put your clothes on.

But she didn't – do anything. It wasn't her fault. It was mine, he is supposed to say. She had nothing to do with it. I was the bastard, and still am. She was innocent, and still is.

Instead, he says nothing. Nothing. At all.

When the headlights of the silver metallic BMW hit the wall of the white garage, the brightness makes everything in the scene seem surreal. It is like the final scene in a play which has been acted out for years, where everything finally makes sense, where everything finally comes together, when the audience watches, with a feeling of regret, the approaching end.

The final stage directions read: philandering husband, rich wife, get out of the car and two doors are slammed. The wife's Versace outfit is stained with tears, the husband's linen suit is as creased as their marriage. They do not speak to each other. The only sound heard is that of their footsteps on the gravel, as they make their way to the front door of their beautiful house.

My dear Linton, the letter begins. And ends.
My dear Lin-, the letter begins. And ends.

The immigration officer at the airport takes a close look at her, then at the photo in her passport, then at her face again. He wonders what is wrong with the woman, whose eyes seem to be so close to tears. He stamps the last page with determination, and hands her the passport. 'Okay,' he says. 'Finish.'

The Sultan's Dream

'Oh, my wives, my many wives, one more beautiful than the other,' says the sultan to himself, when he wakes from his dream. 'Such dreams you give me, of heaven and hell at the same time! Your dark eyes both angels and devils, and your white bodies so smooth, so soft, so tempting … Sometimes I want one and sometimes another, and sometimes when I look at you, in my mouth there is a taste of – how can I explain –'

In the middle of the pitch-black night the famous Sultan decides to call his favourite confectioner. 'Now listen, it's difficult to explain,' he begins. 'I want a sweet as soft and tender as a woman's body.' The confectioner nods. 'But unique,' the sultan continues, and the confectioner frowns. 'It should melt in your mouth and it should stay in your memory like a beautiful dream you never, ever want to forget. But first, let me try and explain. Listen: the melting in your mouth should be slow. Slow, because this woman is like a sweet, she is so sweet, sweeter than the sweetest sherbet you have ever drunk, sweeter than the sweetest love you have ever tasted, sweeter than the sweetest lips you have ever kissed … and slowly you will lick the sugar dust off her body and then gently, very gently bite into her soft flesh, you understand? And then, my dear man, you will chew the most delicious little delight in the world. You understand? Now go.'

The confectioner smiles and bows. 'Oh yes, what a glorious night this will be!' he thinks as he rushes to his kitchen. He understands. He knows exactly.

Yes. Anything for his Sultan. He blends sugar syrup, flavourings, walnuts, fruits, and mixes and tastes and mixes and binds everything together with mastic. After many attempts, the scent wafting in his kitchen is intoxicating and when he licks the sugary sweet concoction off his finger he knows it is just right. He pours it into the tray to let it dry. While he waits, he sits on a chair and daydreams.

'Anything for my Sultan,' he mutters. 'Anything for women and love.' And the Sultan's words make his thick dark lips curl into a smile of lust. 'Lokum,' he says, and when it is dry, he cuts it into little cubes. 'Lokum,' he says to himself again, and sprinkles generous doses of caster sugar on top to cover the perfect flesh he has so skilfully created. The sweet white dust is everywhere, on the floor, on the table, on his clothes, on his hands, on his lips. 'Ah, perfect!' he whispers, and feels his heart beating against his chest fast, faster, faster …

He steps out into the golden sunrise, holding a heavily laden tray. His head held high, he enters the palace and hurries down the softly carpeted corridor … His feet sink into the long silence … He forgets to knock on the ruby-studded door, remembers to balance the tray, and turns the ivory handle:

'Oh great Sultan!' he says, and bows low, one hand behind his back, one hand under the tray.

The sultan is on a divan, reclining against red, orange, yellow silk cushions embroidered with gold thread. The edges of his moustache are as sharp as those of a moon crescent in the sky, and intricate patterns made by sequins on his long robe sparkle like little stars.

'Oh great Sultan!' says the confectioner, and pauses slightly, as if he is about to start reciting an epic poem. 'I present you with the most exquisite little delight in the world.'

Dinner Party

The evening air is like an invisible hand made of silk. They sit together, the four of them, at the table, and the silk air comes in through the open balcony door and touches their faces lightly.

They will remember this evening, this dining room, the blue tablecloth, one day. The beautiful evening in the schizophrenic city, with the breath of spring on the balcony, brought in by a soft breeze. The stillness of the night, at times interrupted by the manic rasp of the delivery boys' motorcycles. They will think back to what was eaten, what was drunk, said, try to remember who said what, in what order. They will try to remember the question marks, the exclamation marks, the commas, the full stops in each conversation, in the same way one tries to remember the details of a painting hanging in the corridor one has passed a hundred times in a lifetime, without paying any close attention.

They will remember this evening, later. The evening of April 1st.

The national holiday meal, the April Fool's day

meal which Helen cooked; Helen and Loizos served; Helen, Loizos, Irene and Christos ate; and Helen and Christos cleared away.

Loizos opens a bottle of red wine, the cork pops. Helen expects the genie to appear and grant her three wishes, or at least one big wish. Loizos says something about the wine-growing areas of Limassol, and the particular region this wine comes from. It is supposed to be a very good wine, according to Loizos, who is a Chartered Accountant, and looks at the label through his glasses which make his eyes look much smaller than they really are, and frowns, which makes him look older than he really is. Helen wishes he wasn't wearing a blue shirt with rolled up sleeves and beige trousers, as if he were at a meeting at work, but a light green polo-shirt and blue jeans, like Christos. One wish already wasted.

After two and a half bottles of the same wine, everyone compliments Helen on her mousakka. Yes, she says, my mother's recipe. The only thing I have of my mother, in her handwriting. It is beautiful, that scrap of paper all stained with oil and her fingerprints (Am I drunk?) I keep returning to it (Please don't, don't burst into tears) and –

She makes herself stop because six pairs of eyes are looking at her closely, and only one person other than herself – Irene – understands. I wish, she thinks, gulping down some more wine. I wish. I wish my mother was still alive. Impossible. Impossible, the throbbing headache tells her. You have wasted another wish.

Irene looks at her and clears her throat and says I'll just stack the plates, if you've all finished, that was lovely, but nobody hears her. Christos and Loizos are doing the usual 'manly' thing and talking about football or politics. One or the other, or both topics of post-dinner conversation, mark the men as two heterosexual, totally normal, perfectly virile Cypriot males, who return, briefly, to their childhood as Loizos arranges and rearranges the salt and pepper pots on the blue tablecloth as if he is reconstructing the match they are talking about and Christos lights a cigarette, puts the lighter on the table and spins it like a little toy. Blissfully unaware of what's going on around them, they talk about the Cup, about Apoel's chances, Omonoia's chances in hell, no way, the way they played like sissies last week? God knows. And all those riots at Tsirion stadium last week, why do you think? Serves them bloody right. Right. Of course it was the referee's fault if you ask me. The bastard should be shot. From where I was sitting, it didn't look like a bloody foul, but the bloody sod gave them a penalty kick, right? Yeah, bloody communists, we're surrounded by them.

More red wine, and the two men are the best of football friends. Finally! Something in common between the chartered accountant, who may or may not be sleeping with Helen, (Christos hasn't decided yet), and the producer from Omega TV channel, for whom the sight of a football even on television means forgetting everyone and everything else in the entire room or even universe. Not such a bad guy this Loizos – even though –

Just shut up, says Helen. Shut up the two of you. You're giving me a headache with this football, football, football – (The effect of the alcohol is making its way to her throbbing head but she knows it is more than that). She is annoyed and drunk and desperate and full and empty all at the same time because this charade has got to stop, she has got to make it stop, these men are cardboard figures, she doesn't know how to reach them, to choose one, to get rid of the other, how to make this scene three-dimensional, fuck you Christos, she thinks, fuck you and your bloody football and nose and lips and mouth, I am a fool, a fool, a fool on April Fool's day. I am a drunken pisshead and a fool. Irene, you too, you're a fool my friend, if you think you can understand him or if you think he understands you, because the only woman who ever understood a bloody man is his own bloody mother.

Agapi mou, I'm sorry, we were only making conver–

What's wro–

Well, let's have some coffee, says Irene. I'll take these plates in.

No. Leave them where they are, says Helen. I'll do the clearing up later. Let's sit on the balcony and play the three wishes game.

What –

What's the three wishes game?

The three wishes game is exactly what its name tells you, explains Helen, trying hard to give an impression of sobriety. We go round the table and we each make three wishes. One after the other. You're not allowed to think too much.

Everyone laughs, sounds like fun, are you sure this is the right time of day or night to be making these wishes, ha ha ha, who's gonna start? Let's get some more wine.

I'll go first, says Irene. Her pale face and white clothes make her look ghostly in the moonlight, and the sight of her sitting across the table from her, looking as if she is almost not there, almost brings tears of drunken bewilderment to Helen's eyes.

I wish I was a natural blonde, says Irene, and laughs. I also wish I could afford a Sri Lankan or Filipina maid. And – I wish – she turns to look at Christos while she says this – I wish I will always be happy.

Everyone claps.

Bravo Irene! Those were good wishes, well-chosen, says Christos, and puts his arm round her waist. Now me. I wish – am I allowed a football wish? he looks at Helen. No, okay, I wish, I wish, I wish, my son will grow up to be healthy and strong. I wish some poor bugger will one day solve the Cyprus problem. And, I don't know, I wish, he says, looking at Helen, I wish life would be simpler.

Everyone claps.

You now, Helen, says Loizos. Ladies first. Because he is nervous, even terrified, at what she might think of his wishes. Perhaps she will laugh, he thinks, and go right off me and the evening will be a total disaster. No, our relationship will be a total disaster, if she laughs. I'm not even funny, I can never make her laugh like this bastard, even though we do seem to see eye to eye in football terms-

No, I'm last, says Helen. It was my idea, so you have to go first.

Right, well, I wish, I wish, you would stop – playing – these silly games Helen (that didn't come out right, no one's laughing). I wish I – could make you laugh. (You couldn't make me laugh even if you tickled me, thinks Helen). I wish I – I wish – I don't know what I wish. This is silly.

Christos and Irene clap, and Helen smiles. Yeah, that's good, she says. Now me. I wish Irene and I will always be friends.

BEST friends, Irene corrects her.

Yes, best, she says. I wish I could speak perfect Turkish.

There is a nervous cough from Loizos, and a silence from Irene and Christos.

And I also wish (this is it) Christos would help me clear up, and do something useful for once in his life.

No, I'll do it, says Loizos.

Are you insulting my husband? laughs Irene. Good for you.

Christos gets up. Okay, I'll do it, but if I break any plates don't blame me.

If you break any plates, you'll have to sweep and mop the floor, too.

It is never possible to predict how a dinner-party will end. Not when everyone is half or totally drunk, half or totally asleep, the guests want to go home, you want them to go home, things have been said which were better left unsaid, things which should have been said were never uttered, and everyone wonders what the time is, when the evening will end and who will manage to get to work on time the following morning.

It is with these thoughts that Helen and Christos carry plates and glasses to the kitchen and put them on the table. It is with these and other thoughts that two people who have known each other for more than four years look at each other's faces in the cold fluorescent kitchen light and think it is quite warm in here (is the oven still on?) ... Why has it gone suddenly quiet as if nobody else exists, as if the two other people have been cut out of the picture, as if they never existed, as if they will never exist again ...

She looks so pretty with her hair tied up like that and her face all flushed and her red T-shirt … He looks so – so –

It is here and now that Helen leans over the table stacked full of plates and leftovers and touches Christos' lips lightly with hers. It is her third wish. It is a mistake. It is wonderful. Why isn't he stopping her? Why does he not stare at her in shock and say something like Listen, this is wrong, what do you think you're doing, I'm married in case you hadn't noticed. Why does he take her face in his hands and kiss her the way she always imagined he would, urgently, as if he is trying to tell her that something he has always wanted to say?

After the kiss, the world wakes up again. The voices of the two others are heard from the balcony, and beyond the balcony, the voice of the city, a distant hum and reminder of reality, of life as it must go on. But two people know something has changed because as the evening ends, an affair has begun.

Good night. Good night.

Helen gives her best friend the Judas kiss.

That was a lovely meal.

The Haiku Writer

Fifty years later he will ask me, do you still write haikus?

There are questions you can't answer. There are poems you never wrote.

There are a million things you have forgotten and a few you remember.

One day in the rose garden you met. There was a smell of fresh roses.

A bouquet of pink.

My favourite flower is the lilac or the iris, not the rose.

The phone rings and I have no strength to pick it up.

It rings and rings. Somebody is trying to tell me something.

I am over thirty and I have no children.

Whoever it is might call again.

Forgot to put the answering machine on. His voice is on it and he is not here. Not any more. It will sound like a ghost. A voice from nowhere.

Last year in winter it was like kissing a man with ice in his mouth.

Do you know what an i-pod is? Sounds like zoology.

Fifty years later we will meet again and he will ask me, why has your hair gone white?

And do you still write haikus?

What's a haiku? Sounds like a jungle animal.

There is that sound like a jungle. A screeching of birds, a screaming of monkeys,

A snake hisses inside my head.

I don't know anything. No one knows anything until the day before they die.

I know that much now.

I used to hate the sound made by crows, that black sound, blacker than bats.

A throbbing in my head.

My hand reaches for the phone, and the minute I pick up the receiver, the person at the other end hangs up.

I laugh instead of crying, and gently put the receiver down.

A beige sofa and another phone ringing, another time, another life.

Let it ring. They'll call again, and his face close to my ear, Let it ring. I want to kiss you. A bouquet of pink roses.

Sometimes things happen before you can stop them.

Let it ring.

Something like a jungle and all its sounds in my head.

A little monkey and its beady eyes, its hairy hands.

Talk to me, little monkey. If you are intelligent. Talk to me.

The clock is ticking in my ear, a slice of silence and a ticking inside it.

There is a small window on the ceiling.

I am counting the syllables for my haiku.

Five – seven – five. Counting.

In the big jungle a small monkey remembers and counts its memories.

What's a haiku? His tongue on my earlobe.

I think I will not wake up tomorrow. I will stay in bed and someone will find me.

Something terrible will happen in my sleep.

I will dream that I am killing myself and I will scream and scream and hope that someone will hear me and wake me up.

The monkeys will laugh in my face and place their palms on my forehead.

They will not know whether I am dead or alive.

They do not care anyway.

They do not care about anything.

Just jump from branch to branch, whistling and laughing.

That's their life. Eating and jumping, whistling and laughing.

Do they ever sleep?

In my sleep tonight I will dream of monkeys.

Fifty years later I might wake up and be in the same room.

In the same room, there is a man I once loved.
We are young again, we are making love.
There are rose petals on the floor.

Ten Nights at the Movies

1. Marlon Brando's T-shirt

It's the white T-shirt I've wanted to wear all my life. Now I have it on, wet and cool on this warm night, the smell of his sweat oozing from it. It clings to my body like a second skin, as if I have just stepped out of an ocean named Desire. I never want to take it off, this white T-shirt which clings to me, white as salt, white as sugar, bitter and sweet, pure white.

Next to me, he sleeps calmly, like a wild wave I have tamed, and whispers in a beautiful dream which I can't see: 'Stella! Stella!'

2. Are Men Ever Honest? Do Women Ever Understand?

'Woody,' I ask, (because I've been thinking about guilty consciences a lot lately), 'Woody, can you tell me why you did that to Mia?'

'Because she never understood me,' is his reply.

I don't know if he's being honest. Probably not. Are we men ever honest about our affairs? 'Do women ever understand men?' I ask him.

'Of course!' he says, looking genuinely surprised, and his eyes look as if they're about to pop out of his head. 'My mother understood me. Even when I was a three-month-old baby she would look at me and nod her head vigorously as I bawled out in Yiddish. Yes, Woody, she would say. Yes, honey, I understand.'

3. Frankly, My Dear …

When we move, this table will move with us. Definitely. Definitely. Yes, this table has definitely got so much meaning for us, so many memories, we have placed so much of our life on it. Mugs and cups of tea and coffee, and all our neighbours, best friends, relatives have sat round it, and all our conversations … Don't you agree? Definitely, no question about it. We won't keep the chairs, but the table must go with us … And tomorrow, remember, we have to look for curtain material. Something light – beige, I think, or perhaps a pastel colour, something like peach to go with the walls. What do you think?

Behind some bold headlines which read GREECE HIT BY BARRAGE OF STRIKES, there is a silence which translates, FRANKLY, MY DEAR, I DON'T GIVE A DAMN.

4. The Cabinet of Dr Caligari

And what if I was the young woman you hid in your cabinet for so many years? What if I grew old never having seen the light, and while I was imprisoned thought that I had a life? What if your experiment failed, and you ranted and raved like a madman the day you opened the cabinet's creaking door and found out I was gone?

5. Psycho

On the landing outside room number 3, the detective pauses and looks at his watch. 2:15 pm. In the meantime a woman is being brutally murdered in a shower in room 15. The detective does not hear her scream as the knife is repeatedly stabbed into the soft, wet, white skin of her back.

The detective is thinking how hungry he is, what a tiring day this has been, how much he is looking forward to going home to his wife and children.

On his way home, he buys a stuffed toy for his three-year-old son. Lately, the boy has been refusing to sleep with the lights off, sometimes wakes up screaming in the middle of the night. Perhaps this stuffed parrot will help, thinks the detective, and starts the car.

6. A few of my favourite things

Getting out of the nunnery, pretending I love children, pretending I am so good with my hands that I can instantly transform curtain material into beautiful children's clothes, pretending to give good advice to love-sick teenagers, manipulating puppets and people, singing Nazi songs, making the Baroness cry, kissing the Captain, and, most of all, having premarital sex with him and getting him to marry me.

7. Here's looking at you, kid

There's nothing I look at more often than this picture of you. It's not even a picture, it's … I know it was taken a few weeks before you died, before I killed you. To some, it may seem sick that I now keep you in a drawer and try to bring you to life, when I could have given you life back then, but didn't, when I could have had you, but didn't. On certain nights, I dream I am giving birth and wake up drenched in cold sweat. It is difficult to explain that I loved you even after they ripped you out of me.

8. L'Avventura

Even the way you looked at me was an adventure. After that, yes, I must admit kissing you, touching you, wanting you, undressing you was the greatest adventure I have ever lived. Love is an adventure film everyone wants to watch. And if somebody were to tell our story back to front, our story would end with a close-up of your eyes looking at me.

9. Bicycle Thief

When will you bring back the bicycle you took from me? And when will you come back yourself? You said you needed to borrow my bike so you could see the world. That you would be back soon, that we would settle down, etc. etc. I sometimes think my bike must be in the most unlikely place on earth, Greenland or Pakistan, Peru or New Zealand, probably because you dumped it there and started to run. So now I need my old mountain bike to ride up all these hills and come and find you.

10. Two Words

She looks at him with big, sad, Ingrid Bergman eyes and holds back tears because she knows. She sees the two words dance somewhere in front of her eyes, somewhere near his mouth, even before he has said them. They look at each other in silence and the two words now fill the whole screen. Is it really? Is it really happening? she wonders. The credits roll, the music plays. She can't believe it has happened. That their life together has reached THE END.

ARMIDA PUBLICATIONS
(member of the Association of Cypriot Book Publishers – SEKYVI)
office | 36a Valesta Street, 2370 Ayios Dhometios, Nicosia, Cyprus
mailing address | P.O.Box 27717, 2432 Engomi, Nicosia, Cyprus
tel: +357 22 35 80 28 | fax: +357 22 35 11 16
email: info@armidapublications.com
www.armidapublications.com